PURGATORY BECKONS

PAUL J BELANGER

Cover concept & design: Paul J Belanger

Published in 2010 by Lost Luggage Studios, LLC
through Amazon CreateSpace.

ISBN: 978-1-936489-00-8

I began writing this book in May of 2005. After you read the first chapter, some may think that I capitalized on the tragic events of Air France Flight 447. This is not the case. My heartfelt condolences go out to those families affected. Most of my writings tend to linger, as was the case with this book. By the time I was finally nearing completion, the unexplained crash of Air France Flight 447 occurred.

I dedicate this book to my father, Jean-Paul. I wish he had had the chance to read it.

A special thanks to my brother, Jamie. His input and editing skills helped me tremendously.

An extra thanks to "Iron Maiden". Their song, "The Prophecy", contains the words "Purgatory Beckons", which always draws my attention. When I conceived this story those words popped out as the perfect title.

-- Paul J Belanger

CHAPTER

1

SOMEWHERE OVER THE ATLANTIC

The Boeing 747-400 was en route from Paris to Miami and was ten hours late for departure due to a mechanical problem with the seal on the upstairs left fuselage cabin access door. Scheduled to arrive at 2:20pm, their new arrival time would be closer to midnight if the winds aloft remained as forecast. Nearing capacity, the aircraft held three hundred and twenty-two people, which included the French crew. It had been a long and uneventful flight and most of the passengers slept as peacefully as they could with the incessant whine of the four engines constantly in the background. Some people were annoyed by it but kept their eyes closed in the hopes that sleep would eventually overtake them, while others found themselves lulled into a droning slumber even though they were in an abnormal reclined position. The few flight attendants currently on duty did barely more than pass out the shrunken white pillows and rough wool blankets or the occasional alcoholic drink for that die-hard businessman wanting to pass the time away in oblivion.

Garrett Carmichael may have been considered a businessman by some, but he never saw himself as such. He reclined his seat as far back as he could, which was nowhere near far enough for his tastes, as he listened to the on board music selection. Bob Seger's "Turn the Page" began and he sighed slightly as he closed his eyes to better focus his mind on the sound and enjoy the song. It was one of his favorite tunes and it always managed to relax him no matter how much stress was found or outright dumped upon him. That one song, on perpetual repeat, may have been his solution to a stress-free life. He wondered if that particular dream was even a possibility.

His aisle seat was midway through the economy section of the aircraft and the seat next to his was vacant, giving him an extra bit of elbow room that he gladly utilized. His ticket was for the window seat but he much preferred the aisle whenever he could get it. It still amused him that the airlines got it wrong almost every time. He knew it was his boss that kept changing it on him just to keep him on his toes, just another curve ball to bump the stress up a notch or two. Luckily it did not take much to convince the aging businessman with the aisle seat to trade with him. The man did not really care where he sat, he was planning on sleeping for the entire eleven hour flight. After the man practically slammed three straight shots of whiskey, in as near to rapid succession as the flight attendants would allow, his trip to sleepy time was guaranteed.

"Now," said the subdued voice in Latin over the earpiece hanging from his left ear. The thin black wire snaked its way down his left side to the small cell phone attached by a clip to the belt on his left hip. The phone had a satellite link add-on since getting a normal cell signal in the middle of the Atlantic was not going to happen. The flight attendant had warned him to turn it off when leaving the gate in Paris but that was never an option, so he broke yet another rule in the rapidly growing list. Despite popular belief, his lack of regard for airline rules did not doom the plane to a crash during takeoff. If crashing a plane were that easy it would be raining metal around the globe.

Garrett removed the airliner headphones just as the song finished, absently tucking them into the pouch in the back of the seat in front of him. He unhitched his seatbelt and stood slowly as he stretched his arms wide and quickly surveyed the cabin. The lights were dimmed and just a few scattered people were still awake and reading various forms of entertainment by the soft glow of their personal lights. They ignored him and everyone else on the plane as Garrett turned to his right and made his way aft.

Garrett stood six feet tall and weighed just over two hundred pounds, most of which were well-toned muscles. Everything about him appeared average, especially his looks and age. At first glance he looked thirty-five but was older than that and with his clean-shaven face the illusion was complete. His dark brown hair was neatly cut and barely curly, almost reaching to his shoulders and completely devoid of the gray that should have been there. He could have been anyone, any-where, and this was one of those times that being an average everything worked to his advantage. He wore clean and black-colored jeans that looked new enough to be considered as such, but were well worn-in and soft and comfortable. His black sneakers had the black shoelaces weaved inside of the laces down the front, to keep them from flopping around. The dark gray button-down shirt with many small light white vertical stripes was tucked neatly into his pants and secured in place by his military style black belt.

He slowly unzipped his dark brown leather jacket the rest of the way and stopped when he caught the glance of a pretty woman seated a half dozen rows behind him. In her mid-thirties, she had dirty blond hair and brilliant green eyes that almost appeared to glow in the dim light of the cabin. As she reached up to adjust her hair the huge ring on her left hand screamed out that she was married, but that never seemed to stop most people nowadays from doing whatever they wanted, no matter who they hurt. He nodded slightly and even managed to make his brief smile genuine as he walked past. She nodded slightly and smiled in response. It felt good to be noticed sometimes but he never liked to make a habit of it. She was seated next to two sleeping children, a boy of about five and a cute little blond girl of almost seven, but Garrett pushed them out of his mind as he continued down the aisle.

"Last row, right side, blue suit coat," said the disinterested voice in Latin. The voice bordered on monotone, with barely enough of a change for anyone to notice. It was usually pure fact, statements with no emotions attached to them and no sense of any urgency either. Only in extreme circumstances would the tone change, and that had happened just once before.

Garrett did not respond, he barely ever did, as he quickly located the man sitting in an aisle seat with the rear wall of the cabin behind him. It was by far the worst seat on the plane since you could not recline and it constantly had traffic passing you on the way to the lavatory. Sometimes a line would even form with people interested in whatever you were doing as they impatiently waited their turn. Flight attendants frowned on people standing and did not allow that to happen for very long. The man was young in comparison and concentrated more on the book he was reading than on his surroundings as he stifled a yawn into the back of his right hand. He had dark hair that was cut closely to his scalp and had even shaved recently, not that he really needed to. The two seats to the right of the young man were vacant, which would benefit Garrett.

Garrett walked past the man, who never even bothered to acknowledge his presence. Garrett glanced back quickly and the man continued to ignore him as he was engrossed in a book about political assassinations, which almost made Garrett laugh out loud and sacrifice his element of surprise. Garrett turned rapidly and grabbed the man by the head, twisting sharply to the right. The neck snapped instantly and the man went limp in his hands as the book dropped to the deck and closed. Garrett released the man's seatbelt and moved the body into the middle seat, sitting down silently next to him.

The snap was a lot louder than he had hoped for and Garrett was relieved as he examined the nearby passengers to see if anyone had witnessed the murder. Nobody noticed or cared, either asleep or close enough to it that it did not matter. Garrett rapidly searched the corpse, looking for a certain something that the Air Marshall was certain to possess. He found the SIG P228 9mm handgun hanging from a shoulder holster under the man's left arm. Garrett removed it slowly and slipped it into the left pocket of his leather jacket as he extracted the two magazines full of 9mm ammunition that were hanging under the dead man's right arm.

Standing abruptly, he straightened his jacket and calmly walked forward, eying the passengers for anyone alerted to his recent actions. He casually glanced at people as he made his way to the forward part of the cabin. He ascended the staircase leading to the upper deck of business class and paused briefly as he surveyed the people seated there. He rapidly walked forward and several businessmen curiously watched him as he passed by them on his way toward the flight deck door.

A male flight attendant ceased serving drinks and blocked Garrett's way. "Can I help you, sir?" asked the flight attendant in French. His hands rubbed together nervously as he stared into Garrett's cold eyes and unconsciously saw something he did not care much for.

"I need access to the flight deck," replied Garrett evenly and in fluent French. It was not very often that he stood in front of someone that made him nervous and this poor man was as far from that person as anybody could ever be.

"Sir, I need to see your appropriate FAA, ICAO, or Air France identification card."

"Will this work?" asked Garrett as he drew the gun with his left hand and placed the barrel against the flight attendant's forehead. Several gasps from those still awake filled the upper compartment as Garrett grabbed the flight attendant by the neck with his right hand. He forced him backward and up against the flight deck door with a loud thud.

"Stay seated," said Garrett slowly and with a brief pause between the words as he glanced over his left shoulder at the nervous business-men behind him. Two of the businessmen talked rapidly in a whisper while they remained standing as they contemplated taking action of some sort. As they turned forward to rush him, Garrett swung the SIG around and pulled the trigger twice, putting a 9mm round into each of their foreheads. The loud popping of rounds being fired managed to awaken the remaining business class customers as both would-be heroes dropped, dead before their bodies hit the deck.

"Does anyone else want to die right now?" asked Garrett as he examined the silent faces in the cabin. "I'm more than willing to oblige you." He swung the barrel of the gun back and forth across the cabin and taunted those that may have considered it. No one else was stupid enough to test the accuracy of his weapon, which he most skillfully dis-played for them, so he returned to the squirming flight attendant pinned against the door.

"Do you have the key?" asked Garrett. He placed the barrel of the gun up the man's right nostril and applied slight pressure, enough to raise the man to his toes.

"No," muttered the flight attendant as he struggled to get the breath out of his compressed throat. His next intake of air carried the acrid burnt smell of gun powder, punctuating the recent deaths.

"All right, we'll do this the hard way then," replied Garrett as he threw the flight attendant into the aisle behind him. The attendant gasped for air while rubbing his throat. He remained prone as he rolled onto his back and watched in muted silence. He coughed a few times as it took several deep breaths before his breathing could return to normal.

Garrett casually knocked on the reinforced door to gauge its strength and heard confused questions being yelled in French from within. A blinking yellow light on the phone mounted to the nearby wall attracted his attention, so Garrett picked it up as he turned to face aft and watch the cabin.

"Hello?" asked Garrett in as mocking a French tone as was possible. He calmly scanned the people in the business class section and assessed their combat value. Most were cowering and praying for salvation while the others watched with morbid interest. The flight attendant sat on the deck, continuing to rub his sore neck but refusing to move from where he had landed. It was the closest thing to smarts that Garrett had seen so far on this adventure.

"What the hell is going on out there?" asked the Captain, in as commanding a voice as he could manage. "I thought I heard gunshots."

"You damn well did," replied Garrett with a reflexive nod. "There are two corpses out here, bleeding all over your brand new and overly expensive carpet, and if you don't open this door I'll make some more."

"Go screw yourself," yelled the Captain as Garrett moved the phone away from his ear. "Kill them all if you like but we'll be landing this plane to a tarmac full of police with your face in their scopes."

"I bet the passengers would like to hear that response," replied Garrett as he gently hung the phone up. Several more businessmen slowly stood and Garrett waved his gun in their direction, so they sat back down with a shrug. He moved the weapon to his right hand and ran his left hand through his hair and over his head from front to back.

"Are you going to kill us all?" asked one of the businessmen nervously from the first row. He was in his late fifties and looked as if his face had not seen a razor in nearly a week. His disheveled clothing spoke volumes on his priorities. Whatever he was selling it must not have been moving very well no matter how much he tried.

"The pilot wants me to turn this plane into a flying morgue and all I want is a better view."

Garrett turned and planted the flat of his left foot firmly against the door, throwing as much of his weight into the kick as he possibly could. The hardened steel door buckled under the force and several muffled

expletives emitted from behind it. Another kick bent the metal surrounding the deadbolt and the voices from within became clearer. The
third kick caused the door to spring open and Garrett shot the pilot in
the back of the head, spraying blood over the left side of the flight deck
and instrument panel. Garrett dodged aside to the right as several shots
rang out from the first officer while the man wildly tried to return fire.
Stray rounds pierced seats and struck several businessmen, sending the
cabin into chaos as everyone uninjured rushed the stairs to get as far
away from the gunfire as possible. One round cleanly passed through a
left fuselage window, sending several small spiderweb cracks out from
the hole that the differential pressure gladly expanded. The next round
fired was followed by an almost deafening click that signified slide-
lock, the first officer's magazine was empty and he had to reload.

Garrett knew his time was running out. He spun around and leaned
into the flight deck to catch the first officer with a shocked expression
on his face as he struggled to insert a fresh magazine into his firearm. A
single round entered the man's left temple and showered the right side
of the flight deck with blood. The first officer's gun dropped to the
floor, the magazine finally locked into place, as the lifeless body
slumped back against the seat.

"Who called out the mayday?" asked the metallic and somewhat
tinny voice in English over the flight deck speaker. "Did anyone catch
that?"

"I think it was Air France 442," replied another male voice on the
frequency.

"It sounded like he said that shots were fired," said a female voice
in quick response.

"Shots fired? Air France 442, please respond," said the controller
frantically.

Garrett pulled the damaged door out of the way and kicked the first
officer in the back, forcing the dead man to fall forward onto the flight
controls. The extra weight on the yoke caused the autopilot to emit a

bing sound as it kicked-off and the plane's nose slowly lowered. As the plane began descending, the dead body's weight shifted on the yoke, causing it to move to the left, making the plane bank slowly in that direction. It would not be long before the momentum was irrecoverable and the plane rolled over onto its back.

Garrett emptied his clip into the glass multifunction displays on the instrument panel, shattering every single one of them. He ejected the spent clip, which bounced off of his right foot and disappeared under the seats, and inserted a fresh one while watching the remaining wounded and screaming businessmen panic behind him. It was becoming difficult to stand upright so he quickly jammed the weapon into the left pocket of his leather jacket and went to the first overhead compartment along the left fuselage. He extracted the pack tucked within and quickly climbed into the two leg straps, putting both arms through the upper straps as he leaned against the bulkhead to steady himself. Then he zipped up his leather jacket and secured the pack's belt around his waist. Further into the overhead compartment was a small black fanny pack, which he placed around his neck so that he would have immediate and easy access to it.

As the plane eased through thirty degrees of bank, the screaming from the passengers became louder as they competed with the increased engine noise. Garrett reentered the flight deck and shut down both engines on the left wing by moving the fuel control switches below the throttles to the cutoff position. He held on tightly with his right hand as the plane rolled over and the graveyard spiral tightened, which made him doubt that anyone nearby was skilled enough to recover from this mess. He watched the backup standard altimeter gauge wind down rapidly as the view out of the front window showed the moon moving in circles about the plane. He was glad that it was night otherwise his stomach might have protested by now.

"Now," said the voice in Latin.

Garrett quickly removed the fanny pack from around his neck and extracted a small black device that looked like a garage door opener as the pack dropped to the deck in front of him. He ducked back further into the flight deck and pressed the button on the remote. An explosion ripped the cabin access door completely out of the left fuselage, taking several more feet of the fuselage with it and causing air to rapidly evacuate from the spinning plane. Several rows of seats and many stunned businessmen were rudely extracted from the airplane into the cold night air. No longer could the screaming be heard over the cacophony of the disrupted airflow exiting the cabin. Garrett stepped from the flight deck into the cabin and was instantly sucked through the gaping hole and into the darkness of a moonlit night.

The last view that the remaining businessmen saw was the face of a man free of emotions whose calm demeanor oddly resigned them to their fate.

CHAPTER 2

PHILADELPHIA PA

Detective Debbie Mason pounded her right fist on the door three times before putting her back against the wall to the left of the doorway. Her diminutive form looked bloated with thirty pounds of protective armor attached to it. Her dark brown eyes were peaceful albeit tired from many sleepless nights of working late trying to track down the individual whose door she stood outside of. Months of work all culminating in this particular moment in time made her more nervous than anything even though the excitement was building in her system.

"Police officers, open up," she yelled as she cupped her right hand beneath the left hand that held her 10mm Glock pistol firmly. She looked to her left and smiled at the other police officer leaning against the wall to the right side of the door. Her eyes were anxious as her lips quivered with reluctant nervousness, increasing more as time ticked by. As often as she had done this she could never overcome that sinking feeling of helplessness, that briefly calm moment just before the mad rush when the assault occurred. She lived for that moment, but in some ways hated it. She never knew if she would ever understand that dichotomy.

Sergeant Jim Maitland held the four foot long battering ram at waist level and waited patiently for the signal. He glanced down the hallway where the remaining members of his SWAT team waited anxiously with their weapons at the ready. For some odd reason he still could not figure out, the pretty detective wanted to be the first person into the apartment. His lieutenant had refused several times before letting Jim make the call, since he was the assault team lead. Jim gave in quickly to those sad brown eyes. He always had a soft spot for women with brown eyes and hers just amplified the word *sucker* written in permanent ink on his forehead. He hoped she would not be the death of him, but all the votes were not in quite yet.

Two shots rang out to break the silence as projectiles exited the doorway at about head level and sank deeply into the opposite wall. The already damaged plaster gave away easily as chunks fell to the floor and an almost white dust drifted down slowly. Debbie cringed as she wondered where the bullets might end up and nodded absently to the sergeant standing to her left. "Not again," she pleaded with a sigh. She whispered a silent prayer as she sank to a crouching position and readied herself.

Sergeant Maitland swung the battering ram at the door just above the handle and the impact ripped the door jam apart. Pieces of wood hung in the air as the door shattered open and Debbie rushed in with the rest of the SWAT team right behind her. Sergeant Maitland dropped the battering ram to the floor while grabbing the MP5 hanging loosely against his body armor and swung it into position.

Another series of rapid shots rang out and one impacted Debbie in the chest. Multiple shots from the SWAT team members replied in unison as the air was knocked from Debbie's lungs. She fell against the wall to the right of the shattered door and sat firmly on the floor while her head slumped downward in frustration.

"Are you okay?" asked Sergeant Maitland as he knelt by her side and tilted her helmet back. She smiled faintly as he examined the projectile lodged in the thick protective armor over her solar plexus. Those damn brown eyes of hers were so sad he would have given her his car if she had asked for it.

"Yeah, I forgot what that felt like," replied Debbie as she struggled to breathe. Her entire chest was sore and it reminded her of a time very long ago when she was playing touch football with the boys on her street. She caught the ball and was running at full steam when someone tagged her forcefully from behind and her legs could not keep up with her forward momentum. Her body fell forward as her legs moved feebly until she met the ground unexpectedly, knocking the wind from her lungs. Was she okay? It took her many minutes of just lying there until she could even speak a response that anyone could understand. Even breathing was laborious and foreign. Just like that time long ago, she could not be angry at herself, she was just frustrated with her incredible lack of luck. It never seemed to change.

"Do you remember now?"

"Oh yeah."

"Good, don't do that again. Okay?"

"I'll try to remember that," replied Debbie as she took a slow deep breath and held it. Her heart ran a race that the adrenaline kept fueling as she leaned her head against the wall behind her. She closed her eyes as her pulse threatened to pop every blood vessel in her head all at the same time. She did not believe there was enough aspirin on the planet to make that headache go away.

"We'll need a coroner on the fifth floor," said Sergeant Maitland into his boom microphone as he quickly surveyed the room they had entered. The apartment was a mess and so out of place for this medium-rent community. If you took the entire room and moved it deep into the slums it would fit in perfectly. But here, the stench of death was present far before the man decided to off himself. Trash lay everywhere and his gag reflex made him wish he had remembered to put the clip on his nose despite having his voice mutated by it. "One suspect down, multiple gunshot wounds, and one self-inflicted fatal round to the head."

"Acknowledged," was the reply over Debbie's earphone.

"Well, Detective, it looks like you got lucky, if you want to call it that," said Sergeant Maitland as he looked down at her.

"I guess it wasn't my time," replied Debbie as she stared at the dead suspect lying in a pool of blood across from her. A part of her mind had seen him eat the barrel of his own gun as several shots entered his torso. But the spray of blood on the wall and window behind him did not justify the agony of failure that she felt. All of that hard work. All of that time spent digging and searching. All of it lost.

"Nope, but if you keep insisting on going in first you're increasing the odds that it will be. Next time I won't let you be the first one in, you will get to be on the sidelines down on the street. Understood?"

"Yes, Sergeant."

"Good."

Sergeant Maitland extended his right hand and helped Debbie to her feet. She holstered her weapon before walking over to the dead suspect by the window of the small apartment. It was dark outside and just after midnight, the end to yet another long day at the office. She sighed heavily as months of hard work lay in a pool of blood on the apartment floor. Had she been quicker, could she have captured him alive? No one would ever know. It was an exercise in futility to follow that line of thought any further than the fleeting moment it appeared in your mind.

"At least this one won't get away," said Sergeant Maitland as he examined the corpse at his feet. The dead man was in his fifties, mostly bald, and had a sick twisted smile on his dead face. He was overweight and ugly and even managed to smell like a rotting corpse before he was supposed to.

Debbie nodded slowly. "I wanted him alive so he could pay for his crimes and spend the rest of his life in jail." All she could think of was the amount of time she had spent over the past months trying to track this criminal down. So many hours of work wasted by a single bullet. But what about the victims? Why were they always the afterthought? She was finding his suicide difficult to accept.

"I like it better when they die," said Sergeant Maitland with a straight face. His honest response mirrored the thoughts of most people in law enforcement, despite their training and knowledge of the law. They were professionals and they did things by the book, but lawyers always seemed to make a mockery of the law that they were sworn to uphold. It was a vicious circle of frustration. "That way the damn legal system doesn't release them back into society."

"The system doesn't do that all the time," replied Debbie as she looked up into the Sergeant's dark blue eyes. She had the same thoughts several times but could not allow that to cloud her judgment or modify the way the law was supposed to work. If she lost that, then what was the point. What *was* the point? She asked that question more often than not.

"No, but once is too often for me. This slimy bastard raped children for years and got away with it, until now. I think he got what he deserved, although being someone's bitch for a few years in prison may have been a better fate."

Debbie was not sure quite what to say in response so she remained quiet as she examined the corpse. The Sergeant had a valid point but it was against everything she strove to be. The entire legal system was already overburdened with frivolous cases of pure retardation as people wasted the court's valuable time with their own personal gains. She knew this dead man was guilty and child molesters never lasted very long in prison anyway. Was it wrong to be glad that one less sickness was present in society? Was it right for her to feel no grief for his death? The only grief she felt was for all the time she had wasted in this man's pursuit.

"Killing them just to remove them from society is wrong," said Debbie as she removed her helmet and held it at her side. Her short dark brown hair was barely above her shoulders and hung loosely about her face. She wore no makeup and her plain facial features had a mildly attractive beauty that betrayed the image she was trying to portray.

"Oh, I don't bust into a room hoping to kill anyone," said Sergeant Maitland while shaking his head slowly. "I'm a professional with a mission to capture criminals that I take very seriously. But that doesn't mean I can't secretly wish for their death."

Debbie nodded as she examined the dead man. He had been fifty-seven years old and gave ugly a new name, and not a very good one at that. He was overweight and had been strung out on methamphetamine, using robbery to fund his habit. Then he added child molestation and murder, leaving a path of bodies for her to follow. It was seventeen weeks of hard work at an end. Not the end she expected but she had to agree with the Sergeant as she contemplated the months or years of courtroom time she would no longer need to be a part of. In an odd way it was a relief, an end. Was it better this way? She did not and could not believe that. There was no doubt in her mind that the legal system was broken and there was no way she or anyone else she worked with would ever be able to fix it. They had to do whatever they could do to work with what they had, which was not very much. That was probably the most frustrating part of her job, the weeks of work being wasted on someone that would never feel the full extent of the legal system. Sure, it was broken. But even a child molester's painful stay in prison, was that comparable to their eternal suffering in the prison of hell? Adding the sin of suicide to that of child molestation, did that increase their punishment in hell? Was anything they could do to that man in this life even going to matter in the giant scheme of things? She had too many questions without answers. The more she thought about it the more she realized the futility of dwelling upon it.

"Want to get a cup of coffee?" asked Sergeant Maitland as he removed his helmet and tucked it under his left arm. He was in his mid-thirties and sported a crew cut, his brown hair still managing to remain free of stray gray hairs. He was very average looking but had a smile that could relax someone almost instantly and he knew how to use it. Jim was a very likable man that made friends without trying. He had a natural charisma that better suited a politician than a police officer.

Debbie nodded absently and followed him out the door and down the hallway. The questions followed her, more likely pursuing her, and she wondered if they would ever stop. Taking a deep breath that caused the pain from her chest to flare up she shrugged, which went unseen beneath her body armor.

CHAPTER
3

SOMEWHERE IN THE ATLANTIC

L eft thirty degrees," said the Latin voice in his earpiece. It was slightly muffled but unmistakable despite the rush of air traveling past him.

Garrett pulled gently on the left handle of his parachute and examined the blackness below. The moonlight glittered on a few waves, sparkling for as far as his eyes could see. It was a beautiful night with just a calm breeze that was lost in the air blowing against him during the descent. At just a few minutes after midnight he still had a lot of work left to do. Sometimes the way things worked out truly amazed him, but he knew that precise planning was the device that allowed him to excel at his work.

He thought of the doomed airliner he had exited a few minutes before and wondered if it had sunk to the bottom of the ocean yet. At that speed and angle of descent the aluminum shell would shatter upon impact with water. There would not be many pieces left to that airplane and recovery would be impossible. No one would ever really know that plane's fate. No one except him, his boss, and their team. He felt no remorse for those that had died, he never did. Everyone dies at some point in life, that was a constant, and he was certain that a time would come when it would be his turn. He would leave this existence without complaint when the time came.

He saw the lights not far in the distance and tweaked his course a few degrees to the right. The position lights indicated that the ship was moving from right to left as he tried to calculate his height and distance to the ship. It was difficult to gauge distance over a body of water, so he concentrated on the ship and made minor adjustments as he approached it. The planning was uncanny and timed to the very second with nothing to be wasted anywhere.

The ship was a British cruise liner on its way to playing in the Caribbean with over two thousand people on her. Garrett adjusted his approach angle and aimed for the midsection. As he neared the ship he pulled down hard on both parachute handles and stepped lightly onto the deck at a walk. He quickly gathered the parachute and removed the pack from his back. He casually tossed it overboard as he made his way aft and to the nearest door. He glanced around and no one seemed to have noticed his odd arrival. Just a few empty chairs existed on the deck as most were stacked aside so the crew could clean up after the day of activities. A couple sat by the pool but were more interested in each other than the man in dark clothing that appeared from the night sky. He casually watched the deck for movement as he closed the door behind himself and continued down the stairwell.

"Faster," said the voice in Latin on his earpiece. *My timing must be off*, thought Garrett as he began jogging down the corridor. He opened the door and entered another long hallway, spotting a crewman wearing a white uniform with rank insignia sewn onto the arm. The man was working on a small panel at the midpoint of the hall, intent on what he was doing. Garrett now knew the reason for the warning message, an unexpected event. Every mission had that potential and they planned for it, quickly modifying events to realign the balance.

"What the hell?" said the crewman to no one in particular as he extracted the strange device. The puzzlement in his voice was a mixture of surprise and shock for finding a device he had only seen previously in the movies. It was a block of C4 explosive with a timer attached, but the time display was not moving and was set to all zeros. Did he find it before it had been set? Could he be that lucky? He caught the movement too late as his luck ran out and the butt of Garrett's gun crashed down on the back of his skull.

The crewman slumped to the floor and Garrett recovered the explosive device. He glanced at his watch and set twenty minutes on the timer. He returned it to its hiding place amongst the electrical conduits and started the countdown as he closed the access panel.

Shattered bones from the crewman's crushed skull had pierced the man's skin and blood had begun pooling under the body. Garrett had hit the man a lot harder than normally necessary but he could not spare the time for a cleaner kill. He grabbed the collar behind the crewman's neck and dragged the corpse into a nearby storage room. There was not much time left to complete this mission so he quickly tossed the dead man onto the floor, closed the door, and continued running down the corridor. Hopefully no one happened upon that corpse before the point of no return, then it would no longer matter.

At the end of the corridor a sign read, 'Engine Room - Crew Access Only'. Garrett did not bother with the handle because he knew the door would be locked. He swiftly kicked it next to the handle and the door bent open as the latch mechanism shattered and clattered its way across the deck. A shocked engineer looked up from his station and the engine noise muffled the shot fired from Garrett's handgun. It entered the engineer's forehead and the man slumped backward in his chair. A quick scan of the room revealed no further human movement so he flipped the safety on and slid the pistol behind the belt at his waist.

Garrett knelt by the door and pried an access panel open to reveal a black duffel bag tucked inside. He removed the bag and slid the zipper from one side to the other. By spreading both sides open he revealed twenty pounds of plastic explosives and a clump of wires wrapped tightly around another timing device. He picked up the bag and stood rapidly. After one last quick glance around, he ran for the engine access door, which would also be locked. He kicked open the door and shot both of the mechanics before they could even turn around to acknowledge his presence.

"Down," said the voice in Latin.

Garrett found the ladder immediately and descended deeper into the depths of the ship. Both turbine engines thrummed noisily above him as he put the bag down and extracted two of the explosive bricks. He quickly placed them and grabbed more to form a circle that was as close to twenty feet across as he could manage in the restricted space. He unwrapped the wiring and placed one detonator into each brick. Kneeling next to the timer in the center, he glanced at his watch and then set twelve minutes on the display. He activated the device and stood slowly while staring as the red numbers decremented their way to their own demise.

"Go," said the voice in Latin.

His time was up and he had to move even faster than before. Garrett climbed the ladder and exited the engine room as fast as his legs could carry him. He found the closest staircase and ascended two steps at a time. As he threw open the door to the deck, a bewildered couple jumped out of his way in surprise as the woman reflexively clutched her man. He ignored them both since they were no threat to him as he ran to the bow of the ship and away from the brunt of the explosives. Most of the explosives lining the ship had been set by another team just days before while at sea. They were a highly competent crew and Garrett never doubted the thoroughness of their work. They were no longer on board but well on their way to their next support mission, and very far from this part of it. When they had a job to do, they did it perfectly.

Just like the waiting parachute and detonator quietly stashed in the overhead compartment of the 747, as well as the explosives carefully concealed into the newly installed cabin door seal.

Another couple moved out of his way with some choice expletives directed at him as he rapidly ascended the staircase to the upper fore deck. A quick glance at his watch showed less than a minute to go for the first phase to kick in. Garrett took a deep breath and glanced to the starboard out of curiosity. The next part of his mission was out there, somewhere.

The muted thump echoed up from the bowels of the ship and Garrett watched as the lights flickered and then went out, plunging the entire ship into darkness. Emergency lighting responded seconds later and left a dull glow in select areas. Garrett turned around and removed the flotation device from the nearby wall. He held onto it firmly as a rumble began shaking the ship. A wall of water shot up from both sides as a large flash of light lit up the sky at the stern of the ship.

Mortally wounded and crippled beyond its capacity to stay afloat, the cruise liner groaned and began its death throes. Explosives had been set alongside the hull on both sides of the ship ten feet below the waterline. The circle of explosives Garrett had set devastated the engine compartment and sent millions of gallons of seawater to flood the entire aft area. Bulkheads designed to isolate flooding were useless when every compartment flooded equally.

The ship lurched and swayed to starboard as several curious people struggled to remain standing. Garrett ran for the railing and leaped into the darkness of the awaiting ocean as the ship pitched up and the stern slid backward into the sea. The ship rolled quickly to port and then upside down. The bow was the only thing left to see as it too disappeared into the silent unforgiving sea.

The odds of anyone else surviving that disaster were slim to none, although Garrett was certain the disembodied voice in his earpiece would be the first to notify him if he had missed anyone. The devastation needed to be total and even those few curious people that stepped into the night air would not have had time to prepare themselves physically and mentally for what occurred next. There should be no survivors here. Both of these supposed accidents, the plane and the cruise liner, needed to be catastrophic and complete. His orders were explicit, his contract exact, and his success rate was as near to perfection as anyone could hope for. That was why he was chosen, because he was thorough and he was the best.

CHAPTER
4

PHILADELPHIA PA

How'd it feel being shot again?" asked Detective Mike Chang as he watched Debbie Mason amble into the office. He was a decent looking man with an unshaven face that screamed of too many hours at work. His brown hair matched his tired brown eyes, showing more age than the rest of his body. He was mostly average in height and weight with just a little bit of extra donut-induced girth. His clothes were wrinkled and may have been identical to what he had been wearing the previous day, or maybe he had never left work since arriving yesterday morning. Either was possible for him. It was almost two in the morning and a few other detectives were also finishing up the day's paperwork and hoping to go home.

"Better than sex," shot Debbie with a smile.

"I'd hate to be your partner."

"Good, let's keep it that way," replied Debbie as she sat at her desk and pushed a large pile of paperwork out of the way. Her desk was a mess and so was her life. There were at least eight large piles of various files and whatever remnants of coffee cups and bagels she had forgotten existed. She removed a small piece of sticky paper with a reminder for her to mail a card to her favorite aunt for her birthday three weeks ago. She crumpled up the note and shook her head with a sigh, having forgotten yet another important thing in her life. Everything had taken a back seat and now the most recent item on her to-do list was to file a report about her role in the shooting of the prime suspect in her most recent mess of a case. All she could do, all she ever seemed to do, was sigh. All of that hard work was lost within a matter of seconds.

"So, the suspect expired prematurely?" asked Mike with a slow nod, knowing exactly what happened. Word traveled fast in this department, and bad news was even faster. He hated losing cases to suicides. It was the most unrewarding part of the job. Sure, the criminal would not commit another crime, but taking the easy way out did not satisfy as much as watching the look on their faces when they realized they would spend the rest of their lives in prison. It was especially satisfying to see that look in child molesters, whose prison stay would be the closest thing to real justice.

"Yeah, self-expiration," replied Debbie absently with a slow and resigned nod. She picked up her pen and scribbled some notes on a pad before opening her drawer to extract the required forms.

"Well, finish up and get some sleep. The Lieutenant wants you to sleep in, show up by noon."

"Wow, I can sleep late? What's that?"

"Wish I knew. Work late, wake early. That seems to be my mantra," said Mike as he pivoted to return to his desk. He looked to the left and to the right and shook his head as he struggled to remember what it was he had been looking for. He compared his desk to Debbie's and there was not that much of a difference between them. He could have seated himself at either and been just as lost.

"Mine too," Debbie mumbled. She began writing quickly as she put down as many facts as she could while her memory of the incident was fresh in her mind. She never even fired a single round this time out, which would be a lot easier on the paperwork than the last arrest she made. That suspect took one round to the upper arm and three to the midsection before he dropped to the ground. EMS was able to keep the man alive for his court date and the jury saw fit to convict him. At least his victim's parents had some kind of satisfaction in the fact that that criminal would soon meet his fate with the executioner. That had to be more satisfying. It just had to be in order for her to keep on the good side of the line. She knew a few officers that had crossed that line and became their own judge, jury, and executioners. Her way just had to make the difference, it just had to.

Debbie finished the second form and dropped her pen ceremoniously on the nearest stack of papers. She stapled the two forms together and paused before dropping the stapler next to the pen. Standing slowly, she walked to the stack of IN boxes lining the wall. Finding the one for her lieutenant, she stuffed the forms roughly into it. She let out a long sigh that she did not realize she had been holding in and turned to exit the quiet office.

Mike gave up on what he was doing and followed her. They were the last to leave the office but he saw no sense in turning off the lights because an early riser was approaching them. They nodded to each other as they passed in the hallway, both too tired to say anything to the other. Mike hit the elevator call button and looked at Debbie's tired and sad face, but he knew her well enough to remain quiet. He yawned absently as the elevator made its way to the ground floor, the quiet between them almost reaching the point of annoyance. Mike opened his mouth twice to say something but opted to keep the silence. When the door opened he watched Debbie walk to her car as he turned right to locate his own vehicle. There were too many nights like this and too many weeks were mirrors of the same.

Debbie entered her apartment and closed the door behind herself, locking it while tossing her keys into an old coffee cup on the table nearby. A growing pile of mail, most of them bills, toppled over to spill onto the floor and Debbie sighed with a yawn as she turned on a small light. She removed her light jacket and dropped it on the floor as she slowly walked to her bedroom. The shoulder holster holding her department-issued sidearm came next and went onto her pillow-filled couch. She undid her belt and began removing her clothing, just dropping things as she went, too tired to not leave a mess. She lived alone so nobody would know the difference and she was too tired to care. Her last live-in boyfriend had left months before, just as her recent case began consuming her life. His biggest complaint was that she loved her job more than she loved him. She could not argue with that fact and just watched him walk out the door. She did not even try to stop him even though he paused to give her the chance.

Her bedroom was dimly lit by the small lamp behind her and she paused as she contemplated visiting the bathroom. She took a deep breath and even the thought of brushing her teeth seemed like more work than she had the energy for. She made her way to the large and lonely bed crowded with pillows. She liked pillows for some odd reason that maybe only a shrink would understand or could explain, and she never cared enough to find out why. It was the least of her worries or concerns. The initial chill on her bare skin as she crawled under her sheets was oddly satisfying as she closed her eyes and exhaled deeply. Her chest was still sore, so she rolled onto her back and pulled one of the pillows over and against her, hugging it firmly.

"Please God, no nightmares," said Debbie to her ceiling. She still believed in God even though she felt the world was heading straight towards Sodom and Gomorrah at full speed. Being constantly surrounded by the bad elements in society, it was taking its toll on her view of society as a whole. She figured that the human race would end up exterminating itself as the bad elements kept increasing exponentially. It was a rather grim outlook on the human condition and there was nothing anybody could do about it. She said a few prayers for the victims of the murderer that she had almost captured, hoping that at least now they could actually rest in peace. A peace that they so much deserved. Hopefully that beast's death was enough justice for them, although society demanded more than a quick end to the criminal's life. Even though the afterlife held its own punishment for that man, she never liked letting them leave this world without paying their debt to society. That was her job and she had to keep telling herself that. It seemed too easy a thing to forget if you gave it half the chance.

She closed her eyes and the tears of frustration and exhaustion hit her as she quietly cried herself to sleep.

CHAPTER
5

SOMEWHERE IN THE ATLANTIC

G arrett heard the droning of the engines long before he spotted the red position light off against the horizon. Mostly obscured and barely identifiable, it was the only thing on the ocean within hundreds of miles of his position since the cruise ship was now located elsewhere. He had no remorse for their lives either and did not think twice about what he had done. His thoughts were focused on the immediate future, a supertanker headed westbound and passing just north of him. He needed to get their attention while they were in range so he removed the small flashlight from his right jacket pocket.

"Now," said the voice in Latin.

Garrett shined the small light toward the ship and hoped for the best. The watertight flashlight, made for camping and water rafting and possibly diving as well, was able to survive depths of up to five hundred feet, according to documentation provided by the manufacturer. He never wanted to test that feature.

"Aft superstructure," said the voice in Latin.

He moved the light from side to side hoping that the flickering movement would catch someone's attention. He kept at it for several minutes until a searchlight lit up the night sky and found its way to his location. Garrett put the flashlight in his mouth and began waving his arms as much as he could until the searchlight locked onto him.

The supertanker slowed, which it would probably do for miles, and a small motorized boat was eventually lowered into the water to recover him. It was difficult to watch their progress as the searchlight remained fixed upon and blinded him. Garrett put his flashlight away and made sure the jacket pocket that his pistol was in was securely snapped shut. The gun was now thoroughly soaked in salt water but there was no way of getting around that in the short time that he had. Being without a working weapon did not bother him in the least. He always considered himself a weapon and the gun just a tool that made killing at a distance possible. It also allowed him to confront more than one assailant at a time, which was becoming more and more common for some odd reason. Every mission was a challenge, that was the one constant that he lived with. No matter how easy a job appeared to be it always managed to throw some bizarre twist in to keep him on his toes.

"Are you okay?" asked one of the men, in Italian, on the motorized boat as it neared him. The man had a girth on him that made Garrett think of the portly seamen that spent their lives on the sea eating that which they were not supposed to. Also mostly drinking whatever alcoholic beverage was the flavor of the week and purchased with their pay once they entered port. The man had a thick graying beard and long gray hair tied back in a clump. His eyes were tired, Garrett's unfortunate appearance probably disrupted the man's drinking binge.

"As okay as one can be out in the middle of the ocean," replied Garrett in fluent Italian. The other man was taller and more muscular but obviously a subordinate to the portly man. Garrett was not sure how he knew that but sometimes a strong impression of people appeared.

"Not quite in the middle of the ocean, but one hell of a long swim to anywhere in particular," replied the portly man. "Are you Italian?"

"No, I just get around," replied Garrett as he accepted the portly man's proffered hand. The other man took his left hand and between the both of them they hauled Garrett onto the small boat. Garrett stretched out on the firm wooden floor and sighed heavily as his body relaxed in relief.

"You have a name?"

"Garrett."

"Well Garrett, I am Mario and this is Giovanni. We are deckhands on the *Sogno di Tramonto*. Out of the Middle East we are bound for Newport News, Virginia."

"Great," said Garrett as he sat up on the floor of the boat and wiped the water out of his hair. He hated that sticky feeling and craved a shower but his mission would give him no time for that for a while yet. "Can I get a ride?"

"What are you doing out here?"

"I seem to have misplaced my ship," replied Garrett as he yawned. He did not need to feign that action but he had no time for sleep either.

"The only thing even remotely nearby on the shipping schedule was a cruise liner," said Mario.

"Well, it's too dark to see anything now," shot Giovanni. He briefly scanned the dark horizon for a ship's position lights, which proved rather difficult with the tanker's spotlight still destroying their night vision. Seconds later he abandoned that futile gesture and shrugged.

"How did you end up in the water?" asked Mario.

"It wasn't easy," replied Garrett with a slight laugh. "I was tossed overboard, by a girl."

"That had to have been one hell of a big woman," shot Mario as he noticed Garrett's strongly built chest through the wet jacket that clung to his body.

The brief inspection by flashlight did not bother Garrett as he smiled widely and chuckled. "Yes, a very large woman," replied Garrett, "with rudders."

Mario and Giovanni burst out laughing and Garrett joined them as the spotlight continued to shine upon them. Mario started the outboard motor and turned the boat toward the supertanker. It was a several minute trip to the stairs running alongside the port side of the supertanker. A man was awaiting Garrett's arrival and assisted him from the boat to the landing. Other sailors helped to secure the small craft for retrieval as Garrett ascended the stairs carefully while gripping the railing tightly.

"I am Renzo, the ship's doctor," said the old man smoking a pipe. He was around sixty years old with gray hair but clean-shaven, although he sported tired eyes from being awakened at this odd hour of the night. He also spoke in Italian and waited patiently for a response, either spoken or visual. Renzo watched the quite waterlogged man ascend the stairs still managing to wear a cheerful smile. Renzo visibly relaxed as he leaned against the railing.

"I'm Garrett," he replied in Italian.

"Ah, Italian?"

"Well traveled."

"Welcome aboard. Let's check you out and make sure you are all right after your little swim."

Garrett nodded absently and followed the man into the depths of the ship. They descended one floor and turned a few corners before coming to the door with a red plus sign on it. Renzo opened it and motioned for Garrett to enter, which he did. It was not a very big room, just enough space for a bed along one wall and an examination table against the other with a gap of about the same size between them. A small porthole was opposite the door and it was closed at this time of the night. To the right of the door was a counter with cabinets containing various medical supplies needed for daily operation. To the left was a tall cabinet with two doors that sported a large lock, most likely to protect prescription drugs for emergencies. Renzo closed the door behind him, locking it from habit so they would not be interrupted, before walking to the counter and opening the top set of doors. He removed a pair of pants and socks along with a thick wool sweater and tossed them onto the examination table. He then took a towel from within and added that to the pile.

"Please remove your wet clothing and sit on the table," said Renzo as he motioned with his free hand.

"No thanks, I'm fine."

"I can't examine you like that. Wet clothes are a good way to catch a cold. Those spare clothes should fit you." Renzo closed the upper doors and slid open the left drawer under the counter. He grabbed the small first-aid kit from within and set it on the counter in front of himself, releasing the clips holding it closed.

"I'm fine, just a little soggy. I'll dry eventually," said Garrett as he rapidly approached the old man from behind. The muffled crack of the old man's neck echoed loudly in the small room, the sound apparently amplified by his desire to bring about a quiet death. A shocked expression on the old man's face stared blankly into nowhere as Garrett slowly moved the doctor to the bed. A quick search of the doctor's pockets produced a ring of keys, which Garrett pocketed. He pulled the top cover off and set the man down onto the sheets before covering him carefully. He turned the body to face the wall and hide the dead man's face from anyone entering the room. Garrett needed time before being discovered and this would suffice.

"Sorry, old man. Your time was up," said Garrett in English. He picked up the towel and proceeded to disassemble the weapon and emptied the three magazines for a proper cleaning. He found a bottle of isopropyl alcohol to clean out the seawater and hoped the gun would operate long enough without oil. He briefly contemplated using Vaseline but did not want to muck up the mechanisms. After the weapon was reassembled he returned the ammunition to the clips, reinserted one, and then racked the slide to put a round in the chamber. He wrapped the two spare magazines with a dry cloth and put them in the right pocket of his wet jacket. He took one of the socks, rolled it on top of itself, then put the barrel of the gun into it. He stuffed the makeshift holster behind his belt, hoping it kept the weapon dry enough to function properly.

He unlocked and opened the door slowly and peered down both hallways, which were vacant. He entered the hallway, closed the door, and began trying keys. His fifth attempt resulted with a satisfying click and he pocketed the keys in case he needed them later.

"Engine room, one mechanic, no rush," said the voice in Latin over his earpiece.

Garrett nodded to a few men that passed him as he descended the stairs. They gave him an odd look when they saw that his clothes were soaking wet, but they did not question him. There was no real use in him changing to the dry clothing the doctor had laid out for him. Although his current set of clothing was wet they were probably going to fit better than the dry set and he needed that known movement factor. Any detrimental restrictions from a new set of clothing could change the outcome of his plan, and that was not acceptable.

From the bottom of the stairs Garrett made his way further into the depths of the supertanker. He had two goals for this mission and the rest would be left to whatever fate had in store for them. The odds were in favor of fate winning this one, hands down, but Garrett never cared much for the odds. He liked having total control over a situation with nothing left for chance. But the boss wanted things this way, it was all part of the master plan with the chips falling where they may. It was not that Garrett was told to perform this mission sloppily, but a few random survivors was considered acceptable for this specific operation.

The engine room door was not locked and a mechanic on duty looked his way as he entered. Not being exactly young, the mechanic was probably in his mid-twenties and must have begun his shift a few hours ago because he acknowledged Garrett's presence immediately. The soaking wet clothing that clung to his body put the mechanic on alert and he grabbed a nearby wrench from the open toolbox.

"Who are you?" asked the mechanic in Italian. "I thought I knew everyone on this ship."

"I am not from this ship," said Garrett as he removed his pistol and shot the man in the head. The mechanic's neck jerked backward and the body paused briefly, allowing the wrench to drop to the deck before the body had a chance to fall beside it like a rag doll. A small trail of blood made its way from the destroyed skull to an open drain a few feet away.

Garrett closed the door and latched it shut. He then found a nearby cabinet and moved it to block the hatch from being forced open. He maneuvered another cabinet so it leaned against the other hatchway at about a forty-five degree angle, allowing him enough space to exit the engine room. Once in the hallway he closed the hatch and the cabinet fell, knocking one of the latches closed and blocking the hatch from being forced open. It was not as secure as the other hatch but would have to do.

"Bridge, three men on watch, two guards patrolling on deck," said the voice in Latin.

Garrett never questioned the disembodied voice's commands or information. It was fact written in stone as far as he was concerned. Most of what he did was reflexive from years of training and prior planning and his dedication went far above and beyond the call of duty. His loyalty to his boss was also unquestionable. If the voice told him to shoot himself in the head, he would, without hesitation or question. But he knew that wasteful order would never come, that was not part of the plan. He liked to think he was too valuable alive and in play, and with his vast experience he was almost at the top of the food chain in his department. He liked the challenge of being in the field so he was reluctant to take the next step in his career path. But, like everything else in his profession, if his boss wanted it, his boss got it.

Garrett ascended the various ladders and paused at the door leading to the main deck. He opened it slowly and scanned the outside area for the roving guards. He saw no one nearby so he exited the doorway and hid in the shadows before a glimpse of movement caught his eye. The guard walked slowly, bored beyond belief and not really guarding anything while taking a drag on a cigarette. One last long pull and the flicker of light arced overboard. The guard watched the cigarette catch the wind and dance in the cool night air. The guard's neck broke quietly and Garrett pushed him overboard, never hearing the body hit the waves far below.

The metal stairs up to the next level quickly passed below him as he approached the next bulkhead door carefully. Garrett put his back against the bulkhead and scanned the vast deck for the second guard but saw nothing. He did not feel like wasting the time tracking that second guard down and knew that the guard would eventually find him on the bridge. It was easier to let them come to you than to go on a bug hunt, and much better in this case to be the hunted rather than the hunter. The primary goal of the mission needed to be maintained and the rest of the pieces would fall into place as they would. That was the nature of the beast and the current beast was him.

After turning the latch, the door opened slowly and Garrett slipped into the shadows within. It was a quiet and long sneak to the bridge as he listened to the voices argue about the first bar they would visit after docking. With each foot placed carefully and cautiously, it took him minutes to cross the same distance that could easily have been covered in seconds at a casual walk. The metal of the slip-resistant deck refused to allow his water-soaked firm-soled sneakers to squeak in warning. The bulkhead leading to the bridge was open and Garrett slowed as he approached it, he needed surprise to be on his side. He drew his pistol and held it at the ready as he leaned around the corner and peered into the open area of the bridge.

The man furthest from the hallway saw him first and gasped as the

first round fired entered his forehead. The loud report of the pistol echoed in the confining area and the following two shots caught the other
two men in various stages of surprise and movement. They never had
time to shout out a warning or to dive for cover. The three bodies collapsed to the cold deck and began creating pools of blood as the ended
lives left their last mark in this world, a bloodstained deck. Garrett returned to the port side entry door and secured it.

"Apply full power," said the voice in Latin. "Two hours and thir-
teen minutes."

Garrett found the power lever and thrust it forward as he looked out
the front window and watched the moonlight glitter on the ocean. There
was no noticeable change in noise nor in motion but the needle that indicated their speed in knots increased slowly. He had plenty of time to
wait before his next action was needed so he moved the three dormant
bodies to a table and seated them around it. He did not need to check
them for life signs because he knew they were all dead, their skulls destroyed by a simple piece of jacketed lead.

"Guard approaching the starboard door," said the voice in Latin in
his earpiece.

Garrett ran to the door and opened it, firing a single round at a
shape in the darkness. A muffled gasp was followed by a body hitting
the deck and rolling down the stairs. He left the door slightly ajar so
that light escaped, a silent beacon to those that would soon follow, for
he wanted them to approach him from here. With the other door secured, even if they attempted to approach from there they would have
to double-back and try elsewhere. There was only one way to reach
him.

The time ticked away as Garrett followed the GPS course-line displayed on the navigation map screen while switching the communica-
tion equipment off. Modern technology made this particular mission
easier. It had been a very long time since he had used a sextant to plot a
course and did not feel like practicing those skills again anytime soon.

He watched the moonlight glittering on the dark sea in front of the ship. Soon he would be seeing the city lights glowing from the United States' coastline. The ship would make it to the pier prior to sunrise, which would aid in his escape. Cameras were commonplace and avoiding them was proving to be a bit difficult. His identity must remain secret for his continued success.

"Two approach," said the voice in Latin as Garrett found himself admiring the moon as it neared the horizon.

Garrett put his back to the control panel and watched the starboard door as the pistol rested behind his left leg. A very long minute went by before the metal bulkhead door opened cautiously. The two men peered inside and whispered nervously to each other. Their hesitation revealed that they had found the body at the bottom of the stairs but they did not know what to expect on the bridge. The first man entered carrying a large wrench while the other followed close behind.

"Who the hell are you?" asked the man in Italian.

"Il creatore del corpses," replied Garrett as he shot the first man in the forehead and put the next round in the back of the retreating man's head. Both men were dead before they hit the deck.

"Creative," said the voice in Latin.

"Sorry. He asked and that was the first thing that came to mind," replied Garrett with a shrug.

Garrett picked up the first of the two newest bodies and put it in the nearby bunk room. The second body was halfway out the door so he recovered it and tossed it on top of the other one. He then glanced around the outside deck for movement and finding none he returned to the controls to wait patiently.

The GPS display showed less than twenty minutes to go and Garrett took over manual control of the ship, adjusting the course slightly to starboard. He leaned his back against the control panel and watched the door as minutes more elapsed. A quick glance over his shoulder showed the coastline approaching rapidly. As the ship entered the harbor, Garrett found himself spending an equal amount of time between watching the approaching lights and scanning the deck for movement. He abruptly changed course to the southwest after passing the Chesapeake Bay Bridge-Tunnel and the speed of the rapid turn caused things to shift across the bridge. The crew still asleep in their bunks would be wide awake now. The supertanker was not scheduled to arrive for another thirty minutes and then they were supposed to remain clear until obtaining a clearance to enter the harbor.

"Go," said the voice in Latin in his earpiece.

Garrett ran for the lowest portion at the aft of the ship, gliding down the steps two at a time using the hand railing. It was quite a run in the early morning after most of the last couple of hours were spent standing around. He flipped the safety on and quickly jammed the pistol into his makeshift holster. He grabbed the aft railing with both hands and vaulted himself into the cold night air. He seemed to hover for a lot longer than he expected as he hoped he was far enough from the propellers when he hit the water. The splash came and Garrett waited for his descent to stop before he removed and released the pistol. He pulled the two spare clips from his right pocket and released them as well. *Goodbye evidence,* he would not be needing them anymore.

He kicked his way to the surface and instinctively turned westward to watch the supertanker in the distance. Seconds later he heard a loud screech of metal against metal echo in the quiet morning hours, and then there was silence. A bright flash lit up the early morning sky in shades of vibrant yellow and orange with touches of red as a fireball expanded from the ruptured carcass of the tanker. Several more rapid secondary flashes erupted as the initial burst of sound finally reached him with the wave of rancid heat soon following. The smell of burning oil caressed his nostrils as the light and flames kicked higher. As random pieces of smoldering wreckage began raining down, Garrett knew that it was time to leave the area. He dove below the surface and kicked his way south to the nearest shoreline.

CHAPTER
6

PHILADELPHIA PA

D ebbie jumped when the alarm clock went off at seven o'clock, in her haste for sleep she had forgotten to turn it off. She hit the clock hard and managed to silence it quickly, but the damage was already done. With her eyes still closed she grabbed the television's remote control with one hand and her pillow with the other. The television came to life as she dropped the controller on the bed next to her and clutched the pillow to her sore chest. The pain was still there and most likely would be for days to come, a subtle reminder of her failure to capture a suspect.

"...And a terrorist attack has not been ruled out. So far the death toll is over one hundred and most emergency crews from the surrounding area are heading to the site. The blaze can be seen for miles around and traffic in the area has been at a standstill. Everyone, please avoid driving anywhere near the Newport News, Virginia area until further notice."

Debbie sat up quickly and grunted as the action of clenching her stomach muscles caused the pain in her chest to flare up and stab into her brain. She stared at the screen in disbelief as the memory of New York was forever forged into her mind. The fire was massive, with flames shooting out of several areas and the black smoke from the burning oil easily turning the early morning sky as black as night. A massive plume of black smoke extended into the slight breeze and into the upper atmosphere, able to be seen for miles. She watched in shock as the emergency crews fought the flames in utter futility, the fire retardant foam only succeeding in spreading the smoke around. Something that huge might burn for days or even weeks before reaching a point of being considered under control.

The information kept repeating as most news broadcasts usually did and Debbie watched in stunned silence. She knew the local law enforcement would have their hands full with people wanting to watch and others wanting to take this opportunity to loot. Crime followed crime whenever it could, usually adding to a catastrophe. To her it was just another indicator among many that pointed to the coming of the end of the world. Everybody hated everybody else and most criminal activity had reached the point of being considered almost normal acceptable human behavior, as twisted as that seemed to her.

Debbie turned off the television with the remote and slowly rolled out of bed. Her sore chest demanded her attention and she rubbed it absently as she walked into the bathroom. She turned on the shower and stared at her naked self in the mirror. Her hair was a mess and the bags under her eyes did not make her very appealing, no wonder she was still single. The black and blue marks on her upper sternum, where the trauma plate had been forced against her skin, was the icing on the proverbial cake. Why did life always mean pain for her? Sure, her job was considered dangerous but that did not mean that good things could never happen. Did it? She asked that question all too often and never seemed to find an answer, only more questions. As the steam fogged up the mirror she was glad to be hidden from her overly critical eyes.

The water was hot and Debbie reveled in the relaxing liquid as she let the stream beat against her still sore chest. The massaging action of the shower head eased the soreness and allowed her to take a deep breath, which she exhaled slowly. She took a longer shower than normal and dried off absently as she ran yesterday's events through her mind. Did she do everything she possibly could have to capture that deviant child molester and murderer? The more she ran the events through her head the more she realized that an answer she liked may forever elude her. Nothing was ever easy and nothing was ever straightforward.

Debbie dressed slowly and collected the clothes she had dropped around the apartment in her haste to get to bed. Overall the apartment looked lived-in. A big couch with more pillows than most people ever see in their lifetime dominated the living room. An average-sized television and small stereo were the extent of her entertainment center. Several CD jewel cases sat next to the television and were from bands that were popular two decades ago. A small bookcase contained books on firearms and criminal psychology alongside other books she kept from her college days, like algebra. Why did she keep that? Most likely because she had not had the time to spend sifting through all the garbage she had collected over the years. She really needed to do some spring cleaning no matter what season it was. She probably could have kept her apartment cleaner with less in it but she never did seem to spend that much time at home anyway. She realized that she had missed a lot of things in life because of her job, but she enjoyed her job, which was more than most people could say. Her last boyfriend and all the previous ones never could accept that, and thus the relationships fell apart. Two months was her record for the longest relationship, and three days was the shortest.

The phone rang, shattering her thoughts of the past and bringing her back to reality. She grabbed her shoes and sat down on the couch with a grunt from the pain in her chest. Debbie dropped the shoes on the floor in front of her and answered the phone on the third ring. She rubbed her right temple with the first two fingers of her right hand while closing her eyes.

"Hello."

"Debbie, what are you doing up?"

"You woke me up, Mike," said Debbie as she slipped her left foot into a brown shoe.

"Bullshit," replied Mike with a snicker. "When I wake you up it takes at least ten rings. That's how I know you are sleeping."

"Are you keeping notes on me?" asked Debbie as she tried to tie her shoe one-handed and gave up. She tried to balance the phone on her shoulder with her ear pressed against it and almost dropped it several times before finding the proper spot. She leaned forward and grunted slightly as she quickly tied the laces.

"I've got a file," said Mike with a short laugh.

"So, what's up?" asked Debbie, quickly changing the subject. She knew Mike liked her and wanted a relationship but she would never let that happen. She did not want to date anyone at work, and with her track record she was reluctant to date anybody anywhere. She did not need the grief nor the awkwardness after the relationship with a co-worker was over, which was a constant in her life. Lately she subconsciously doomed every relationship before it ever had the chance to even begin in order to save time for the inevitable result later on. It simplified the entire dating process.

"Did you see the news?"

"Unfortunately," replied Debbie as she discovered that tying the laces on her right shoe proved to be a bit more difficult than with the left shoe. She had to start over twice before she could complete that early morning task. "What a mess. Looks like a supertanker ran aground at full speed with a full load."

"No, not that, although it is pretty bad but we've got ourselves a new serial killing spree on our desks. Three prostitutes on the same street, all killed the same way. The Lieutenant wants us on this one right away so get your pretty little ass down here."

"My pretty little ass doesn't do anything you ask it to do. Haven't you figured that out yet?"

"I keep hoping."

"Well don't. You're a good detective and a good friend and I don't want to ask for a new partner, so let's just keep it professional, okay?"

"Okay," replied Mike with a soft sigh. He really cared about her more than he was willing to admit to anyone, including himself. "What's your ETA?"

"I'll be out the door right after we hang up."

"So get going."

Debbie did not bother answering him, she slammed the phone down and stood as quickly as the pain in her chest would allow. She checked her weapon and grabbed her keys, taking one last look around before shaking her head and opening the door.

CHAPTER
7

PORTSMOUTH VA

G arrett watched in silence as the fires continued to burn
across the bay, sending a plume of black smoke so far into
the upper atmosphere that airline flights had to divert
around it. It was a lot further swim than he expected and a lot longer
than he was ever used to. His arms and legs were sore and his clothes
were soaked with his hair a sticky kind of wet that was more annoying
than anything else. He really wanted a shower but would settle for a dry
change of clothes. He turned away from the carnage and proceeded to
the nearest parking lot in order to acquire a vehicle. He had one more
big part of the mission to complete, followed by a little bit of waiting,
then he needed to disappear until the excitement dwindled. Then, in
time, he would prepare for the next big mission needing to be done. In
all his years of life this particular mission was the most activity in the
shortest amount of time. He found it interesting and exhausting both at
the same time.

"Red truck," said the voice in Latin in his earpiece. It amazed Garrett that with all the swimming he had done in the past several hours that the thing was still attached to his ear. Especially after the long drop from the deck of the supertanker into the bay. Add on top of that the drop from the deck of the cruise liner and that was two plunges too many. That never even took into consideration his skydiving adventure. It was a well-designed earpiece.

Garrett found the red pickup and scanned the parking area as he approached it. Other than the inferno across the bay it was a peaceful morning and the parking lot was vacant. The truck was a Chevy with faded red paint and a splattering of rust along the entire bottom of the side panels. The driver door sported a large rusted dent with flaked paint indicating it was a recent addition. It was unlocked and opened with a screech and a few pops which dislodged several rusted metal pieces that fell to the ground. The interior looked just as abused as the exterior did, with the fabric of the seat ripped in several places to expose the stuffing held within. After a brief search of the immediate area he found the ignition key hidden under the ripped carpet near one of the seat posts.

The truck started easily and belched a cloud of bluish smoke that indicated oil leaking into at least one of the eight cylinders. This truck was beat to hell. Garrett was surprised the thing still ran and expected more pieces to fall off before he got to where he needed to go. The fuel gauge indicated three quarters of a tank of gas and he hoped it was accurate. That should be more than enough to get him to his next destination; Petersburg, Virginia. Garrett placed the truck in gear and grunted when the transmission chattered in protest as some gears ground themselves further down. One good bump and that poor truck just might burst into flames. He backed up and carefully shifted into drive while waiting for the grinding to stop. He headed south to find Route 460.

Once outside of Norfolk, the traffic subsided and it did not take very long before he made the swing to the northwest. He began rolling down the driver's window until the handle came off in his hand and the glass dropped and shattered behind the door panel. He tossed the handle on the floor in front of the passenger seat and opened the rear middle window to get some airflow so he would eventually dry off. The brisk morning air was refreshing and Garrett yawned absently as he settled into the traffic flow behind a BMW.

As he approached a small town the traffic increased. Time went by and Garrett found himself being annoyed by the frequent rapid movements from accelerator to brake pedal. Now knowing this truck, he fully expected his foot to go right through the floor one of these times.

As society grew up he found that it became less and less considerate to others. Everyone was out for themselves and cared not a wink for anyone else. Garrett grunted as he was forced to slam on his brakes to avoid hitting a small blue car that cut him off. The car had racing stripes and a large racing vane on the rear trunk, and the music was so loud that Garrett was certain his heart stopped beating every time the bass rumbled. Another feature which he found completely stupid were the various fake bullet holes along the trunk.

"Blue car," said the voice in Latin over his soggy earpiece. As the saltwater dried on his skin the earpiece became a permanent part of his ear. "Bad day."

"Thank you," replied Garrett with a smirk. He was going to enjoy this more than he was supposed to. People like this annoyed him because they were so self-centered.

Garrett waited patiently for the perfect opportunity to present itself, as he knew it soon would. This part of his job was an art form to him and he excelled at it. It took a tremendous amount of skill to ruin someone's day without outright killing them. Although death would be the ultimate way to ruin someone's day it was over instantly. Just giving someone a bad day in his line of work meant that the recipient needed to live to experience their newfound grief. That way it stayed with them for a lot longer.

The blue car's brake lights came on and Garrett hit his brakes a fraction of a second too late. The red truck's poor brakes struggled to lock up and eventually his tires screeched on the pavement as the blue car approached rapidly. By now the other driver realized what would soon happen, but in this backward society the accident would not be the blue car driver's fault. The red truck tapped the blue car's rear fender, mostly marring the plastic lining. The impact was just slightly above that which the bumper was rated to handle without showing damage. It caused the music to skip a few beats and then cease briefly until the CD player could reset itself.

The blue car's door opened rapidly as Garrett opened his door and quickly reached behind the seat. He found what he was looking for almost instantly and ran his hand over it until he found the hard plastic grip.

"You fucking moron," shot the young punk as he examined his rear fender. There was no real visible damage to the car but he did not care. With just a few scratches on the dark blue plastic bumper he was planning on making a much bigger issue of it than necessary. That was something else that was becoming the norm for most people in a so-called free country. They were free alright, free to protest everything and hate everybody, and society suffered for it. "Can't you fucking drive?" he almost yelled. The punk was in his late teens and had more grease in his dark black hair than brains in his skull. He wore black jeans and a white tank top with a chain around his waist. Various tattoos showed on his arms and neck and part of a tattoo on his chest was mostly hidden by his shirt. Garrett realized instantly that this punk was some kind of gangbanger, which made this much more interesting.

"I'm sorry," replied Garrett as he eased his door closed and kept both of his hands hidden behind his back. "You shouldn't have braked so abruptly."

"Fuck you," yelled the punk while pointing his middle finger at him. "I'll kick your ass."

"Nice bullet holes," said Garrett as he motioned toward the blue car's trunk with a nod of his head. He had no idea what the purpose of fake bullet hole stickers were, just something else he found stupid in society.

The punk looked briefly at the fake bullet holes in confusion before returning his stare to the calm man standing in front of him. The man driving the red pickup truck had no idea who he was dealing with. He had beaten people to a bloody pulp for much less than this guy had done. The punk reached into his back pocket and produced a butterfly knife, quickly flipping it open with a flutter of metal against metal.

"Let me touch those up a bit," said Garrett as he swung the 9mm Uzi from behind his back and racked the slide to load a round into the chamber. The black strap dangled from the two mount points to oscillate as he firmly grabbed the front grip to steady the weapon.

The young punk dropped the knife and backed up quickly as he waved both hands in front of himself. "Whoa, man, it's cool. Don't hurt my car. I've got a lot of money in this thing. I was just joking, okay? We're cool, man. We're cool."

Garrett counted four fake bullet holes at odd intervals across the back of the car's trunk. He expertly squeezed the trigger and placed a single round rapidly into the center of each one. The plink of the jacketed hollow point rounds hitting metal echoed against the buildings, causing several people to run for cover while others watched in silent amusement.

"Shit!" yelled the young punk as he cringed in sympathetic pain. "My car!" His poor car was being violated by a crazed madman in a beat up old red pickup truck. That was what he got for traveling this far from the city.

"There, that's a little bit better, but there's still something missing." Garrett stepped to the side of the car and raised the weapon once again and pulled the trigger. He placed a few single rounds into the left rear quarter panel. Traffic was stopped by this time and most townspeople watched in silent satisfaction as their morning evolved.

"Stop! Please stop!" pleaded the young punk to deaf ears. The madman was not listening.

"Don't like my upgrade?" asked Garrett as he pointed the weapon at the punk's midsection. The young punk found what brains he had left and took off running in the opposite direction. "I guess not. Maybe a little bit more will help," yelled Garrett as he switched to full automatic and returned his attention to the blue car. He held the trigger down and the clip quickly emptied as Garrett showered the entire left side of the car with bullets, the spent shells bouncing in tiny tin echoes on the street next to him. He then reloaded and dumped a second clip into the car to destroy all the windows for good measure and mostly because the punk had pulled a knife on him.

Several bystanders began clapping when the loud music ceased and the car began spewing steam from the busted radiator, spilling its fluids into the street like the blood of a dying beast. Garrett nodded in satisfaction as he returned to his truck and carefully tossed the Uzi on the front seat. He put the truck into drive and slammed into the rear of the small blue car, pushing it to the side of the road and out of everyone's way. Then he sped off before the police had time to respond to a shooting incident and waved goodbye to the stunned punk standing on the sidewalk.

CHAPTER
8

PHILADELPHIA PA

The alley stank, but it was not from the three dead prostitutes lying on the ground in front of her. The smell was a cross between vomit and urine with a touch of garbage thrown in for good measure. The alley itself ran straight from one main street to another with a niche of about twenty-five feet wide by twenty-five feet deep. The three dead bodies occupied the ground in that area, neatly out of view from either street and only spotted by the morning trash collectors. Two large dumpsters sat in the corners and were still piled high with trash as the trash truck waited for the police to finish looking the area over and questioning the two men. Had the murderer or murderers waited just one more evening they could have tossed the corpses into the dumpsters and may have gone unnoticed for days, or forever for that matter. Dead rats or dead bodies, they stank pretty much the same when it came down to it.

"This place reeks," said Debbie to no one in particular as she tried to get the stink out of her mind. She stood next to one of the prostitutes and kept her left hand in her pocket while her right clipped her nose closed.

"It smells like my ex-wife's house," shot Mike with a snicker. He had a small pad out and was making notes of everything he saw whether important or not. It saved his ass in court more than once because the lawyers always dug deep and would argue the finer points of your memory in the hopes of getting the case thrown out, and their high-paying criminal client set free. By having it all written down you left nothing committed completely to memory.

"Your ex-wife was a prostitute?" asked Debbie before she realized it. She usually tried to remain professional but Mike liked to screw around all the time and that comment caught her off guard.

"Nope, a whore. She never charged."

Debbie smiled as she removed her left hand from her pocket and knelt to examine the three dead prostitutes. All three of them took a small caliber round to the back of the head and only one of them had an exit wound. It was the classic assassination scenario. She glanced around the immediate area and found no shell casings nearby, which was odd but not unheard of.

"No casings?"

"Nope," replied Mike as he scratched behind his right ear with the back of his pen.

"Did anyone see anything?"

"Nope, too busy hiding in their own private worlds, ignoring everything else."

"Great. Another blank slate to work from. No leads, no clues, and no ... hello?" Debbie removed her pen and pried open the fingers of the young blond girl closest to her. In her hand was a pack of matches from a nearby gentleman's club, *The Spared Eagle*. The story behind the name was one of stupidity on the sign maker's part. It was supposed to have been *The Spread Eagle* but a typo changed things, and neither party could come to an agreement for correcting it. So the name stayed and the lawsuits continued for years, and was still stuck in the legal system. Many years and dollars later, much more money had been spent than that stupid sign was even worth. Neither party was willing to drop the case and admit fault.

"Ah, a clue," said Mike with a quick laugh, "we're halfway there."

"Maybe. At least we have a place to start, and hopefully we can ID these bodies." Debbie knocked the matches into a Ziploc bag and sealed it. She examined the other two bodies to see if anything out of place screamed for her attention but found nothing else. The dead sometimes told their tales as if screaming and at other times it was just a whisper. Occasionally they said nothing at all.

Mike and Debbie spent the next two hours gathering and labeling the evidence and personal effects of the three young women. They walked the alley several times looking for anything else of interest, but found nothing. The killer, or killers, were thorough and that would make their job a lot harder.

With the grim duty completed, they returned to the station to re-search records for any further clues or direction. They would have to wait at least a day until the coroner could perform the autopsies and hopefully get fingerprints or dental records that actually existed in the database. As they entered the office, the rest of the detectives were gathered around the television set and listening intently.

"Whoa, they've got porn again," shot Mike as he quickly joined the group gathered around the television set.

"Not even close, just CNN," said Leo Teller, their tired lieutenant. He stood nearly six feet tall and might have been a linebacker if he had any muscles. He spent too much time in a chair and not enough on an exercise machine, trading barbells for donuts. He needed to purchase new shirts to match his growing girth, but refused because that would be acknowledging his rapidly growing waistline. Denial was always the better option and as active as the department was that seemed to be the better argument.

"CNN? What gives?" asked Mike.

Debbie approached her desk and sighed heavily at the large pile of papers scattered about. She had thought she moved most of the big piles out of the way but more had populated the recently emptied space. She really did not know where to begin to clean it all up and figured she would just put it off for some other time. She just needed enough room to work on this current case and the rest would have to wait.

"CNN is having a field day with this one," said Leo as his cup of coffee traveled to his lips. He took a sip and groaned in relief and pleasure because someone had made it extra strong again. He needed to use his detective abilities to discover who that person was, so he could thank them with a raise. "First there was a missing plane, then a missing cruise ship, and now a crashed supertanker. No terrorist organizations have stepped forward to claim anything but many have been suspect. Some people are blaming the damn Bermuda Triangle, and UFOs too. Crazy bastards with nothing better to do."

"Hey Lieutenant," shot Jim Burke, "they got the ship crash on video, check it out."

The poor quality video displayed the ship entering the Bay and making a rather sharp, in shipping terms, left turn to aim for Newport News. It was early morning and someone driving across the Chesapeake Bay Bridge-Tunnel with a camera decided to record the event. Maybe it was the speed at which the ship went by that had caught their attention and caused them to record the event. It was difficult to tell exactly what went on during the video as it shook and the city lights flickered. It made Leo's stomach protest and he had to close his eyes to recover from the discomfort.

Then the ship grounded itself by crashing into some kind of lit structure, maybe the pier itself. The lights went out and the camera steadied as the person taping it must have rested the camera on the railing and zoomed in for a closer shot. The burst of orange-yellow flames caused the view to go from twilight to day in a fraction of a second. A billowing blackish cloud of smoke obscured the flames until the video camera shook violently when the sound finally reached the small microphone. Someone off camera yelled, "Holy Shit!", before the censors had time to catch it. Leo was sure that it would be edited out for the next broadcast.

"Damn," said Mike as the word stretched out to at least twice its normal length. He watched the replay silently while his comment was echoed around the department as others shook their heads slowly in shock. It was the World Trade Centers all over again. "Imagine all the paperwork," shot Mike. Some laughed while others protested the grimness of his joke.

Leo shook his head and sipped his coffee before he turned to his office. "Get back to work. Someone please arrest somebody today. We need to catch some bad guys."

"Yes, Lieutenant," responded the group as they turned off the television set and returned to their respective desks.

Debbie opened the case folder and began making notes of all the little bits and pieces she had discovered. It amounted to next to nothing, so close that there was no difference. She sighed and thought of all the other cases that began with the same lack of clues. It was too soon to tell if this case would be solvable. She would give it a week before making that determination.

"Where to next?" asked Mike as he pulled up a chair and sat down next to Debbie and smiled. She was a plain looking woman, the kind that most men never noticed, which was the boat that Mike had been in. It took him over a year of working with her until one day it dawned on him that she was plainly beautiful. Once that line was crossed he found himself being drawn to her more and more as time went by. She avoided makeup and always dressed like a man, mostly because the job required it. It was difficult to hide a gun and run while in a dress and high heels. The thought of her wearing a dress and tackling a suspect made his smile grow even wider.

"What are you smiling about?"

"The futility of this damn job. Do we stand any chance of solving this one?"

"The votes aren't in yet. I'll give it a week before depression sets in. Besides, none of these damn cases would ever be solved if we gave up only half a day into the investigation." Debbie ripped a blank sheet of paper off the pad on her desk and began writing down a list of paths to follow. The most obvious being that they could hit *The Spared Eagle* and see what they could dig up there. Then it would be a depressing walk down memory lane with the girls' families, if they could even find them. Their list was small, but it was possible that one of those four paths would open up even more doors.

She remembered a case a few years back where all she had to go on was a receipt from a hotel where you could get rooms by the hour. No name and no credit card numbers. All that was on the receipt was a date and the time. That led to a description, which led to a pimp, which led to a long list of adult stores. One by one they made their way around the city until a friend of one of the dead prostitutes along the way knew a first name. Then things got messy and the trail of bodies led to the suspect. He shot himself in the head, but lived and found his way into the legal system. Luckily all the laws were followed perfectly and this particular scum entered the prison system. The last news that Debbie had read from prison reports was that the man was a very large black man's bitch. The killer had spent untold hours in the infirmary for various contusions and several failed attempts at suicide. Hopefully he lived and suffered for a very long time to come. As far as she was concerned, that was justice.

"Okay, let's hit the strip club and see if we can add to your list."

"You're gonna like that," said Debbie with a short laugh and a smile that brightened her face. Her deep brown eyes glimmered and caused Mike to catch his breath. She was a truly and simply beautiful woman.

"Didn't say that I wouldn't. I couldn't tell you the last time I saw a real live naked woman."

"As opposed to a fake one?"

"Yeah, fake as in pictures. But, then again, most of the women in strip clubs are fake too. They're all hiding from something, which usually includes themselves."

"I didn't expect that level of revelation to ever come from your lips," said Debbie, with a look of shock on her face. Maybe she underestimated this man.

"I am getting older. I guess the wise-ness has to come out some time."

"As opposed to wise-ass?"

"Hey, you do know me!"

"All too well. Let's get to work."

"Yes ma'am."

CHAPTER
9

WAKEFIELD VA

G arrett glanced at his rapidly diminishing fuel gauge and turned into the nearest gas station. He thought it would have been enough fuel for the trip but this old truck had more issues than a stripper. 'Thirty gallons to the mile' was a line in a catchy tune he remembered from a band that he managed to see play once. He pulled up to the pump and wondered if he had enough money in his pocket. A quick search of his person revealed nothing at all. He searched through the glove compartment and under the seats but again, nothing.

"Inside," said the voice in Latin through his earpiece.

Garrett figured from that command that the solution to his dilemma was in the store. He did not really feel like robbing the place and then standing at the pump filling up as the police arrived, but sometimes that was part of the plan. He could never just do what he wanted unless what he wanted was part of the plan, and it was not his place to determine that. His place was to act and react as was necessary, as he was told.

He opened the door and entered the small gas station mini-mart, immediately analyzing the combat value of the two occupants. A young girl of perhaps sixteen stood at the counter arguing with the attendant. Her brown skirt was too short, revealing way too much bare leg, and her white shirt barely covered her top as it left her midsection bare. Garrett slowly walked down an aisle and feigned examining the merchandise while checking the rest of the store out. There were no other patrons and only a single emergency exit down a nearby hallway. Garrett watched out of the corner of his eye and waited, neither person posing a threat or concern.

"Come on," pleaded the young girl, "I've got the money."

"But I need to see some ID," replied the attendant.

"It's just a pack of Marlboro Lights. It won't hurt you to let me buy them."

"But it's against the law. For all I know you are wired and there's cops outside waiting to bust me for contributing to the delinquency of a minor."

"Shit," said the young girl as she sighed and began walking around the store. "Maybe I'll just buy some candy instead."

"*That* I can sell you," said the attendant.

"Very funny."

Garrett carefully paused at the end of the aisle as the young girl approached him. Her childish face confirmed to him that she was around sixteen, if that. She had a small gold crucifix on a thin gold chain around her neck and wore black eye shadow along with bright red lipstick. In a different city she would be a prostitute, but Garrett doubted that was the case in this small town.

"Hey mister, can you buy me some smokes?" the girl whispered while looking over the candy selection.

"I have no money."

"I can pay for them."

Garrett decided to take this opportunity. If Garrett let her leave without taking her money then he would probably need to kill the attendant and take the gas, which left a trail more apparent than the blue car. While either option was a viable solution, the quieter path was usually the best to choose, and kept the authority's focus elsewhere. That was the important part to his mission, keeping the focus somewhere else until he was ready to attract it. So the lesser path was his first choice and the best choice. Besides, he had a timetable that he had to keep so his decision was made for him long before he even entered this store or situation.

"I need gas money," said Garrett evenly. He did not care much for helping this young girl destroy her body with the toxic sticks but it was not his place to either accept or deny her. It was her choice and hers alone.

"Here's a twenty."

"No. Buy some candy, little girl," said Garrett loudly as he accepted the money and winked at her.

She sighed audibly, stomping her right foot on the ground like a spoiled brat, and stalked off while grabbing a package of candy cigarettes from the nearby shelf. "Will you let me buy *these* cigarettes?" she loudly asked the attendant while holding the package up.

"Sure will," said the attendant with a snicker, "as long as you promise not to choke on them."

"Everyone's a comedian," said the girl as she approached the attendant and threw her money and the candy cigarettes on the counter. She adjusted her short skirt that kept managing to ride up and threaten to reveal more than just her legs.

The attendant rang up the candy cigarettes and handed them to the girl with her change. "Have a nice day," said the attendant with a smile and a snicker.

"Yeah, right." The young girl exited the mini-mart and stopped outside to open the package. She pulled out a candy cigarette and stuck it in her mouth, blowing out a candy-simulated puff of smoke. She then turned her head toward the attendant, extracted the cigarette from her mouth, and stuck out her tongue at him.

"Cute kid," said Garrett as he approached the counter with a candy bar and the twenty dollar bill in his hand.

"Yeah, I get them in here all the time. It gets old very quick."

"I also need a pack of smokes, Marlboro, and the rest for gas for the red truck out there."

"Regular or the Lights?"

"Regular," said Garrett as the man reached for the pack behind the counter. "Um, better make them Lights. I really need to quit."

"I quit three years ago. Going Light won't really do it for you," said the attendant as he glanced at the young girl outside. She was walking toward the phone at the north end of the station parking lot. She did not look back as she slowly skipped across the pavement.

"It's the thought that counts," replied Garrett. He followed the attendant's eyes to see the young girl skipping away.

The man handed him the pack of cigarettes and rang up the gas sale. "The pump is turned on for you. Have a nice day."

"You too," said Garrett as he opened the pack and pulled out a cigarette. "Got a light?"

"Shit no, man. Not while you're fueling. You wanna blow the place up?"

"Maybe," replied Garrett as the attendant shook his head with a sigh. tucked the cigarette behind his right ear and exited the store as he slid the pack into his pocket. The young girl was on the phone and never glanced in his direction. If she had any sense whatso-ever she was watching the reflection in the metal plate on the phone.

Garrett pulled the handle from the pump and stuck the nozzle into the fuel receptacle. It did not take very long to put fourteen dollars and change into the thirsty truck. It better be enough to get him to Petersburg. The way this truck sucked down gas he wondered if there was a giant hole in the gas tank. The odd thought forced him to look and luck-ily there was no stream of gas pouring out.

The young girl left the phone and began walking down the street to the north. Things could not have been going smoother for this illegal transaction. Garrett was surprised at how good an actor this young girl was. Her disinterest was so well staged and out of character for some-one so young. Most people would have remained right in the parking lot so that the attendant, and nearby cops, would easily see. No one said there were no cops watching from elsewhere, but the odds of that hap-pening were low. He had no choice in the matter either, he needed to complete this drive intact.

Garrett started the truck, shifted it into drive, cringed as the gears ground some more metal off of themselves, and left the gas station behind. The young girl glanced back and waved as he approached. He could have just stiffed the girl and kept going, hoping she learned a valuable lesson, but he would not do that, unless specifically told to. He was a man of honor and besides, he owed this girl at least the cigarettes for putting gas in his tank. He slowed to a stop and the young girl opened the door and hopped in. She had a big smile on her face as she slammed the door shut and struggled to roll down the window. She then noticed the window handle on the floor by her left foot and kicked it out of the way.

"I thought you were gonna take off."

"I thought about it, but I was glad you didn't hang around the gas station and wait for me."

"Gotta make him think he was successful," smiled the young girl, revealing more wisdom than someone her age should have. "What's your name?"

"Garrett, how about you?" He handed her the single cigarette from behind his ear and then the pack. He then stepped on the accelerator and began driving down the road.

"Trace, as in Tracy." She pushed in the cigarette lighter and waited.

"How far are you going?"

"Petersburg," replied Garrett.

"Oh, how were you planning on paying for the gas if I hadn't shown up?"

"Not sure, maybe with this?" said Garrett as he pulled the Uzi out from behind the seat. The young girl's eyes opened wide and her jaw dropped as her mind told her to flee.

"Shit, can you drop me off at the next corner?"

"Sure," said Garrett as he slowed down and brought the truck to a stop next to the curb. The lot was a vacant hole in the ground where a building would one day stand and bring cheer to all those around, at least that is what the sign said.

The lighter popped out and the young girl quickly lit her cigarette and then jumped out, slamming the door shut behind her. She leaned into the open window and smiled as best she could manage while still being within range of the Uzi. "Thanks for the cigarettes and the ride."

"No problem. Thanks for the gas money."

"I stole the money from my parents," said Trace with a shrug. "Thanks for not killing or raping me. Or raping me and then killing me. Or killing me and then raping me."

"Not part of the plan," replied Garrett with a straight face. "But do try to stay innocent for as long as you can. Once you cross that line there's no turning back."

She shot him a weird look and Garrett nodded. He pulled away from the curb and watched her staring at him in the rear view mirror.

"Nice try," said the voice in Latin.

"I just hope she listens to me."

"Not likely," replied the voice.

It was the nature of the beast. No one ever listened to him even though some sure seemed like they would. He learned a long time ago not to care about anyone he met but sometimes he felt like trying be-cause that was his nature. His boss understood and did not mind when things moved in a direction that gave him the opportunity to try again. It was a fruitless effort though, but they both knew that he had to at least try, for that was who he was.

"Train leaves at 3:51pm," said the voice.

Garrett looked at the digital clock on the radio. It was barely noon so he had plenty of time, as long as the truck held together for him, which was not as likely as he wanted. He would much rather have hours to wait at the station than to be late by even a single minute for an appointment. He could not miss that train, no matter what.

CHAPTER
10

PHILADELPHIA PA

*T*he *Spared Eagle* opened for business at noon. Several businessmen waited in line outside for the doors to open, many of them wearing suits. The place served lunch but most of them were there for different reasons. They all examined Debbie closely as she walked up to the front door with Mike by her side. She banged on it several times with her clenched fist and waited patiently. The men undressed her with their eyes, hoping that they were seeing a coming attraction. She caught their looks and rolled her eyes with a disgusted sigh. None of them realized that the working girls went in the back door and not the front with the patrons.

"We open in ten minutes," said the deep voice loudly from within.

"Police officers," said Debbie as she watched several of the men slowly disappear. She almost laughed out loud as their embarrassment exceeded their need to see naked women.

The door opened slowly and Debbie and Mike flashed their badges in unison. The large man, made mostly of muscle, inspected their badges with a keen eye and then opened the door widely, motioning for them to enter. He stood roughly six feet tall and was built like a line-backer for just about any football team you could think of. He was clean-shaven with a high-and-tight haircut of light brown hair and bright blue eyes that seemed out of place in such a large muscular man. His biceps were so large and defined that Mike cowered and felt insig-nificant standing next to the man.

"Come on in, Detectives."

"Thank you," replied Debbie as she entered the currently brightly lit establishment. She hated these places, hated what they stood for, and hated how women could do this to themselves. She had talked with enough strippers to know the money was really good but the lifestyle they inflicted upon themselves was not. She had no respect for any of these women, or the men that frequented these places. They were just as bad since they drove up the demand for women to bare themselves. The entire stripper world fed into the prostitution world which rolled into the drug world. One feeding off the other, fed the other, and another until the entire crime market was one giant feeding frenzy of money and depravity. With all of that gone she might be out of a job, which was perfectly acceptable to her.

"Is the manager in?" asked Debbie, wanting this entire trip to be over as soon as possible. Every breath reminded her of her recent mis-take as the soreness in her chest flared up. She had another hot date with her shower planned and wanted to begin immediately.

"Not yet. Should have been here by now but must be running late. Can I help you?"

"We found at least one of your girls dead in an alley this morning. We were hoping to identify one or all three of them if we could," said Debbie as she turned to face the big man.

"Three? Dead? Shit. How?" asked the bouncer as he stepped be-hind the bar and grabbed two glasses. He placed them on the bar as he looked Debbie in the eyes. Something about her screamed for help but he just could not place it. He had a weird feeling run down his spine and his senses instantly became alert, scanning the immediate area for threats. That thought gave him even more chills as the memories from a life long past surfaced and the fighter instinct in him took over. Something bad was coming.

"Shot in the back of the head," said Debbie as she opened the folder and laid out some pictures of the three girls.

"Want something to drink?"

"Not me," said Debbie.

"I'll take a Coke please," said Mike. The bouncer nodded and filled a glass with ice and Coke.

"Her I knew well," said the bouncer as he pointed to the redhead. A look of sincere sadness crossed his face as his response began a bit choppy. "Cherry Lemonade was her stage name. Real name was Linda Parks, if my memory is right. I liked Cherry, she ... was my favorite."

Mike made notes on a small pad while Debbie kept watching the bouncer's face for alternate clues. Sometimes a lot of their job was reading faces and expressions. This usually told them a lot more than the words coming from their mouths did. Some people only spouted lies and tall tales that rivaled skyscrapers in magnitude.

"Could you tell us anything else about her?" asked Debbie.

"Eighteen, from Idaho. Boise, I think. Ran away from home was what she told everyone. I never believed much of anything the girls said to anyone though. Most of these girls lie for a living and a lot of what they tell the guys they eventually believe. She was friends with the blond. They hung out all the time. Her name was Candy Lace, well, her stage name was. That's what they want to be known as. It makes things easier for them, so they can distance themselves from themselves. I think her real name was Sharon Burrows."

"What about this third one? The brunette."

"Seen her once. She hangs out with some real rough types. Those guys are major assholes. I got into it once with one of them. He grabbed a girl's ass and that's a no-no in here. You cops stop by all the time and we don't want to lose our liquor license, so we crack down on that shit."

"Yeah, yeah, spare us the legal disclaimer," said Debbie as she waved her hand dismissively. The laws were only followed like every other law in society, when the people enforcing them were there to see you.

"He's right, Debbie," said Mike. "The guys I know that stop by said this place stays legit. Been that way for over a year now, unlike with the last owner."

The bouncer nodded and topped off Mike's glass. "The safer we keep this place the more patrons we get. Sure, we lose the ones that break the rules, but it has paid for itself. Lose one, gain a dozen."

"So what happened with the asshole?" asked Debbie.

"I got up in his face and he started yelling at me in some other language. Then he opened his jacket and showed me a gun in a shoulder holster and I backed off. The manager went over and talked with him for a while and I ended up having to pay for their drinks all night. That sucked."

"What language?" asked Debbie.

"Not sure. It was a Makarov pistol though."

"Are you sure about that?" asked Mike.

"I don't know languages, but guns I know. Trust me on that."

"How long ago was that?"

"A couple of weeks. I usually see them here every night, and avoid them, except they weren't here the last couple of nights."

Debbie looked at the pictures and wondered how they all tied together, or if they did. It seemed too easy for those foreign guys to be the ones involved in this, but sometimes things worked that way. After the last case she struggled with, it would be nice to have something simple and straightforward. She felt that she deserved it. "Did these girls ever hang out together?"

"Tanya, that's it," shot the bouncer as the glow in his eyes reflected the glint from the light bulb of recognition going off.

"Tanya?"

"Or something like it. The third girl's name. Yeah, the two dancers seemed to really like that girl. She was a heavy drinker and always had a lot of money to throw around. She really liked watching girls dance and usually spent money on table dances from both of them."

Mike's eyes lit up with renewed curiosity.

"Shit," said the bouncer as he looked at the clock. It was a couple of minutes past noon and he ran around the bar. "Hang on, let me open up or I'll get my ass chewed."

Mike took a sip of his Coke as he sat down on the bar stool. He watched Debbie flip through the pictures as she scrunched up her nose in thought.

"What do you think?" asked Mike.

"I think we need to see if we can find those foreign guys. But there's no way in hell I'm gonna be seen in this place again for any reason. And I'm not gonna pretend to tend bar or go undercover as a dancer here either. No way."

"Aw, come on Debbie. You could easily be on stage here."

"Mike, cut the shit, I don't want to hear it."

"Okay, sorry, bad joke." He straightened his back knowing that he had pushed too far. He was infatuated with her but she was all work and no play with him. There was nothing he could ever say to get her thinking about him. Mike did not know why but he wanted to be with her. The more he tried the further she pushed him away.

The silence was broken by the music coming on as the lights dimmed and patrons entered and found seats. A waitress exited the back room and approached with a pad and pen to take their orders. The bouncer checked the ID of every single person without looking back at the two detectives at the bar. Debbie believed the bouncer's stories, his mannerisms were in line with his eyes and words. He just seemed so out of place in this strip club.

"I'm sure several of the guys in the department will gladly stake this place out tonight and every night until they find those foreign guys."

Debbie laughed, "Yeah, and I'm sure you'll be right there with them."

"In mind but not in person. We've got some work tracking down whatever friends and families we can locate for these girls. I think Tanya will be the tough one to find out anything about."

"I think you're right."

"Sorry about that," said the bouncer as he returned.

"No problem, you've got a job to do and we're only in the way," said Debbie as she looked the big man in the eyes. There was a depth there in those deep blue eyes that intrigued her. They were both strong and sad at the same time.

"True, but Cherry was really special to me. She reminded me of my little sister, so ever since she got here about six months ago I have been going out of my way to be like a big brother to her. I doubt she appreciated it, probably thought I was like everyone else and just trying to get into her pants. So if I can help you find who did this to her, you've got it. Especially if you need some skulls cracked, because I can do that too. Maybe a little wall-to-wall counseling to loosen them up before you question them?"

"If only our legal system would allow that," said Debbie while still staring into his vibrant eyes.

The big bouncer sighed noticeably and nodded reluctantly. He knew not even that would bring Cherry back to life. It would only make the painful reality less painful for him, for a little while at least. "Do you have a way I can reach you if I think of anything else?"

"Sure," replied Debbie as she produced a business card and handed it to him.

"We'll have some undercover cops in here for the next few nights to see if those guys show up. We'd really like to talk with them," said Mike.

"Have the undercover guys talk to me when they come in. The name is Kurt but most call me Sarge."

"Sarge?" asked Mike.

"Marine."

"Currently?" asked Debbie.

"Naw, retired. But once a marine, always a marine."

"Well, Sarge, it was nice talking with you," said Debbie as she extended her small hand. Sarge took it in his large hand and carefully shook it.

"Glad to help. Hope you find those that did this."

"We will, it's just a matter of time."

Debbie turned and headed for the door as Mike finished his drink. He followed her out the door and waited for her to start the conversation. She was not forthcoming though and they were halfway to the station before he had to break the silence.

"Do you think he was telling the truth?"

"No doubt in my mind," said Debbie. "It was in his eyes."

"So, now what?"

"You said it earlier. We'll get some of the guys to stake that place out and we'll dig into the lives of these girls to see what we can find."

"It's always the same," said Mike with a big sigh. "We dig and dig in the hopes that we find the secrets that lead us to the killer, or killers."

"Mike, do you like your job?"

Chapter
11

Petersburg VA

G arrett abandoned the poor red truck in the Amtrak parking lot with the keys still in the ignition. With any luck the truck would be stolen and miles away from the station by morning. It did not really matter though. It was not time for him to cover his tracks just yet. Once this mission was finished he would disappear until needed again.

He entered the busy Amtrak station and approached the ticket window on the left side of the room. There were three people in front of him so he waited patiently as the Uzi hung under his right arm, hidden by his jacket. He had only one clip left, and two empties in his jacket pocket, but it would have to do until he could get more ammunition. His clothes were mostly dry now, except for his sneakers, and he still yearned for a shower. He avoided touching his still sticky hair, because he knew that would annoy him to no end.

"How can I help you, sir?" asked the ticket agent as he barely looked up. The bored look on his face showed that he had been on duty for a very long time and no longer cared. The caffeine having long since worn off, there was nothing left to keep his concentration as he watched the second hand on the clock across the room. He sighed forcefully and stifled a yawn before looking back down at the book in front of him.

"You should have a ticket for Michael Gray on the 3:51pm train to Philly."

"Let me check, sir," replied the agent as he turned to the stack of tickets awaiting pickup. He thumbed through the pack and eventually found it about halfway through the pile. "Here it is. Well, this is odd."

"What is odd?" asked Garrett.

"It has a picture of you attached to it. I guess you don't have an ID?"

"It was lost in the Atlantic, along with the rest of my things. I haven't been home yet to get a replacement."

"Ah, and this gets you home?"

"For the time being."

"Oh, hang on a second." The agent walked to his desk and found a key attached to a note with Garrett's fake name on it. He returned and handed both over to him. "The key comes with it. Maybe some clean clothes?"

"I certainly hope so. I smell like a drunken fisherman."

"You said it, I didn't," replied the agent with a slight smile.

"Thank you, I think," said Garrett as he accepted both and turned away. He really was beginning to smell like a dead fish that had been in the sun far too long. He could not find a shower soon enough for his tastes.

He put the picture of himself into his right front pocket and ripped the note and string from the key. He placed the note into his pocket as well, for disposal later. The lockers were down the hall and he easily found the one he was looking for. A blue suitcase waited for him within. He took the suitcase from the locker and found his way to the nearest restroom.

The restroom was empty so he opened the door to the last of four stalls on the right side and placed the suitcase on the toilet. He closed and latched the door then opened the suitcase to reveal a set of fresh clothes and sneakers along with a clean jacket. He removed the picture, note, and two empty clips from his current jacket pockets. He quickly stripped, hanging his Uzi from the hook on the stall door. He tossed his old clothes onto the floor and quickly put the fresh clothes on. The Uzi came next and was followed by the new jacket. He pocketed the items and exited the stall with the suitcase, placing his old soiled clothing into a trash receptacle. He splashed some fresh water on his unshaven face and ran some through his hair to remove as much of that sticky feeling as he could. He grabbed the suitcase and left the restroom for the waiting area.

The waiting area had at least six dozen people scattered about waiting for various trains. A quick scan of the area revealed an old man sitting alone and smoking. Garrett sat down next to him and nodded at the man. Garrett pulled out the note and picture and rolled them into a small tube. The old man eyed him curiously as he puffed casually on his pipe.

"Got a light?" asked Garrett of the man.

"Sure," said the old man as he pulled a lighter from his left breast pocket. "Here."

"Thanks," said Garrett as he leaned over to the ash tray and lit the tube. He watched it burn until he could no longer hold it and dropped it into the awaiting ash tray. He waited until the rest were ashes then he handed the man the lighter back. "Gotta destroy the evidence."

"Always a good idea." The old man nodded and quickly stood and left, deciding that he did not care to know what kind of evidence or for what it pertained to. Some things in life were just too much information and this was one of them.

Garrett looked at the clock, he had almost an hour to wait. He put the suitcase between his legs and leaned back in the chair, closing his eyes briefly as he listened to the sounds around him. The station was noisy from all the people talking and the various announcements coming over the loudspeakers. Some people loved to travel but Garrett found it a means to an end. For the most part, travel meant work for him. When it was time for another mission it involved travel, and travel always brought disaster.

It took only a minute for him to focus his mind and thoughts on the cacophony of sounds around him. He spent some time isolating them but could only pick out a few words here and there.

One voice kept getting louder but in the surrounding din he could not make out which language it was. It definitely was not English, that much he was sure of. The woman was adamant about something and obviously her point was not being understood. He wanted to turn around and find the cause of the disturbance but he resisted the urge. He opened his eyes and settled them on the clock to see that not much time had transpired.

"Help her," said the voice in Latin.

Garrett stood and picked up his suitcase. He walked with a purpose directly to the old woman at the counter, avoiding several people along the way. She was wearing all black and was at least seventy years old, maybe crossing the border into eighty. As Garrett neared her he recognized the language as Czechoslovakian.

"Can I help any?" asked Garrett of the agent.

"Not unless you speak Polish."

"Not Polish, Czech, and I do."

Garrett turned toward the old woman and spoke in perfect Czechoslovakian, "Excuse me, ma'am. Can I be of assistance?" He nailed the dialect and accent, which shocked the lady into silence. "Are you alright?"

"Sorry, young man. I didn't expect anyone from Prague to be here. That is where you are from, right?"

"No, I'm just well traveled," replied Garrett.

"Oh, well, nice to hear a voice from home whether you're from there or not.

"My husband has passed away and my niece has a ticket here waiting for me to go to Washington DC. He was there on business for the government and staying with my niece for a few days. It was his time, I'm afraid. I'm not much looking forward to this trip. I must pick him up and return here for the funeral. Such a sad time."

"My condolences, ma'am. It is a sad business. I will help you get your ticket. What is your name?"

"Alzbeta Madzik. Thank you."

"Sir," said Garrett to the agent in English. "Her name is Alzbeta Madzik, and she has a ticket waiting for her. She's going to Washington DC."

"Okay, I'll check." He searched the same pile and found the ticket close to the bottom. He did not bother asking for an ID since the odds of another individual fitting the name and circumstances was just too far fetched. "Sorry for the confusion, ma'am," said the agent with a sincere look on his face.

Garrett relayed the agent's words and the lady thanked him, which he also translated.

"Safe journey," said Garrett after he showed the lady where to find her train.

"And to you young man, thank you."

Garrett nodded and returned to his seat while staring once again at the clock. Time for his train neared and he ran the next part of the plan over in his mind as the minute hand moved slowly forward.

CHAPTER
12

PHILADELPHIA PA

I love this job," said Bill Dunne while watching the naked woman dancing on the stage. Yet another short blond girl whose hair looked as bleached as the desert of White Sands, New Mexico. She was barely eighteen and must have spent some money having her breasts enhanced. They were at the point of defying gravity, so firm that they were probably as solid as the girl's skull. That was an odd thought and he wondered if the girl could claim them on her taxes as a business expense. It must have been possible in situations like this, but then she would probably have to account for all of the tips as well.

"Remember why we're here, Bill," said Jim Burke. He was the younger of the two and was recently married and enjoying every minute of it. Finally at twenty-five years old he luckily was not the youngest man in the department, but was very close. His full head of brown hair made Bill's balding head stand out. The two of them looked like opposites, Jim standing much taller than Bill. Bill also refused to exercise and it showed, whereas Jim ran three times a week and worked out every day. Jim found himself admiring the scenery, it was rather nice but duty came before pleasure and he knew his wife was going to have a fit when she found out about this stakeout. She would find out too. She always did.

"Yeah, but it has been almost three hours with no bad guys showing up. Oh damn, look at that redhead. Oh, yeah, this just got better."

"You're a dirty old man," shot Jim with a snicker as he sipped his Coke. He watched the redhead walk across the floor and stop at a nearby group of old men for a table dance. She was wonderfully built, thought Jim as his mind wandered.

"Don't get out much, eh?" asked Sarge as he set down another glass of Coke and a Sprite for Bill.

"Nope, too busy working," shot Bill as he contemplated drooling over the redhead. She was an incredibly beautiful girl, a little bit older than his daughter. That made him pause in his current train of thought as reality woke him up when Sarge continued speaking.

"Well, speaking of work, you may want to watch the three that just walked in. That's them. The guy with the leather jacket is the leader of the bunch, or so it seems as the other two keep looking to him before doing anything." Sarge left them to ponder this information as he returned to the bar with a tray of empty glasses.

The leader was nearly six feet tall and had a bulging midsection from overindulgence. He wore black pants and shoes, with a black leather jacket over a black shirt. Nothing shiny anywhere except the expensive watch on his left wrist of which the diamonds caught the strobe light and flickered back in synchronicity.

The other two men were taller than the leader and also a lot more muscled. The first one stood behind the table the leader had chosen and scanned the room, either looking for someone in particular or categorizing the patrons. After the leader was seated and the other guard had positioned himself to watch the door, the standing guard sat down and relaxed.

A young brunette with a tray holding three glasses and a bottle of clear liquid approached the table. She set the tray down and filled a glass before handing it to the leader. She then filled the other two glasses and gave them to the guards. She left the bottle on the table and as she turned to leave the leader pinched her ass. She flinched but kept walking, saying nothing nor changing the expression on her face. It was the kind of scene which irked Jim. The typical rich bastard that thought he could get away with anything. They usually abused the law whenever they could and never thought twice about caring who was hurt in the process.

"I'll call it in," said Jim while standing and forcing himself to sway a bit. He did not glance in their direction, fearing that the guards might be more alert than they appeared. He made his way across the room and carefully edged around several performing girls in various stages of nudity. His wife would have him in the dog house for weeks after this. It was going to be a rough few weeks if he was lucky.

Jim entered the restroom while removing the cell phone from its holder on his right hip. He flipped it open and hit the key sequence to speed dial the department. It displayed as 'Uncle Leo' as the call went through.

"Philly Homicide," said the female voice on the other end.

"Debbie?"

"Yeah. What's up?"

"It's Jim. We've got company."

*

"On my way. Thanks." Debbie leaned over and hung up the phone then grabbed her jacket from the back of the chair. She glanced around the room and searched for Mike in the group of people gathered around the television watching CNN.

"Mike," said Debbie loudly.

Mike stood slowly while shaking his head and pointing to the screen. "That's all kinds of messed up." The others agreed as he walked up to Debbie.

"They're at the club. Jim and Bill will keep an eye on them. We've got to hurry," said Debbie as she headed for the door with Mike following close behind.

They entered the parking lot and Debbie unlocked the doors to her blue Ford Taurus. It may have been old but it still ran just fine and got her where she needed to go. She did not have the time to find another car and really did not need one or care to deal with any salespeople. After climbing in she started it up on the first crank and pulled out of the lot. It was not a very long drive and she had hoped for silence, but Mike was a talker.

"CNN is talking about conspiracy theories with the plane, cruise liner, and supertanker accidents. Air Traffic Control reported that other pilots heard the pilot of the downed airliner say that shots were fired. Then the damn plane's crash site was along the course the cruise liner was on. Where the cruise ship disappeared is almost in line with the tanker's course. The entire FBI staff has been working around the clock on this one. Surprisingly, no one has claimed responsibility. How's that for freaky?"

"Yeah, freaky," said Debbie, hoping for silence. She needed to think about a course of action to handling these individuals. It would be either really smooth or really messy, all happening in a heartbeat. She hoped it was the former but usually it was the latter.

"What's your take on it?"

"I don't care," replied Debbie coldly as she made a right turn. "I've got to concentrate on this case."

"Come on, show some sympathy. People have died in the thousands for this one."

"I'm concerned with us and our friends at the club right this moment. The rest of the world can fend for itself."

Mike sat there staring at her as the lights of *The Spared Eagle* grew in the distance. Debbie was a lot quieter than usual and it not only an-

noyed him but concerned him. She would typically involve herself a bit
more in his rants, albeit antagonistically. Mike eased his handgun from
his holster and checked that a round was waiting in the chamber. His
10mm Glock felt comforting and he wondered if this simple interrogation would turn ugly. Sometimes the thought of a gunfight excited him,
but tonight it seemed a lot more like work than anything else. He silently slid the weapon back into place and snapped the restraining strap as
they pulled into the parking lot full of vehicles.

Debbie had to park way in the back, in a dirt area under some trees.
A few men were standing by their car having a smoke as she opened
her door and glanced in their direction. The conversation stopped and
both men watched her in silence as Mike followed her to the club.

"I'll go in the back way," said Debbie as they approached the establishment. The music inside was loud and she could not only hear it but
feel it as well. The techno track was heavy on the bass and even heavier
on the annoyance factor. "Wait until you see me by the restrooms before you approach them."

"Right. Do you think this will go the easy way or the hard way?"

"Hard," said Debbie with a sigh. "Very hard."

A shiver ran up Mike's spine and for the first time in a very long
time he was scared. Debbie had a very good head on her pretty shoulders and had almost a sixth sense when it came to reading people. Sure,
she had read the last sicko wrong but sickos had the tendency of being
unpredictable.

Mike opened the front door slowly and was greeted by a blast of
smoke-filled hot air as he got into line. Sarge was standing against the
wall checking everyone's ID. When Sarge recognized Mike he waved
him through with a nod.

"They're still here," said Sarge as he looked in askance at the door,
waiting for Debbie to appear. The look in his eyes ripped something out
of Mike that he could not explain but felt right to the bone.

Damn it, thought Mike as a wave of jealousy formed in his heart.

He likes her too.

"Debbie's going in the back door," said Mike reluctantly. She had already told him multiple times that there was no interest there. But part of him still hoped, and would always hope.

"Okay," said Sarge with a nod. He caught the look in Mike's eyes, the electric fire of jealousy with a mix of rage. "Watch yourself around these guys. They are unstable and have been drinking Vodka for about half an hour now. Also, they are packing."

"Still three?"

"Affirmative."

Mike entered the club as Sarge motioned to the man behind the bar. The man changed places with Sarge so he could better see what was about to transpire. It was both a morbid curiosity and a professional interest which urged him to watch. All the girls that worked here were like family to him, and his duty and honor to protect them drove him to help as much as he could. He would have felt more comfortable behind an M-60 machine gun, but that was at home.

Mike saw Debbie in the alcove and approached the table with the three men. He caught Bill and Jim's eyes and they reached into their jackets in silent and expectant anticipation. Mike removed his badge from his shirt and let it fall to hang by the chain at the middle of his chest.

"Gentlemen, please excuse me, but can I ask you a few questions?"

"You interrupt us, go away," replied the leader as the other two men sat straighter in their chairs. The tension in the air thickened immediately as the two men appeared as coiled and ready for attack as snakes. Arms folded across their chests they could easily have their hands on weapons.

"Do you know any of these women?" asked Mike as he tossed the pictures of the three dead girls onto the table.

When the pictures hit the table it took just a fraction of a second before the table was upended by the second guard. The guard with his back to the wall produced a MAC-11 and racked the slide as Mike re-acted instinctively. He dove for the nearest cover as bullets filled the air he had just occupied. The second guard also produced a MAC-11 and targeted Bill and Jim as they extracted their firearms.

Between the music, screaming, and gunfire there was not much of anything that anyone could make out. The cacophony was punctuated by smoke and bloodied bodies filling up the club. Jim was the first to return fire as he put three well-placed rounds into the second guard's chest. The guard fell backward into his chair, falling over it and was dead before he hit the floor.

Mike took a stray round to his left calf. It went in and came out the other side, sending a sharp pain straight to his mind. He struggled to get further away from the bullets being sprayed in his vicinity as several sent chips of wood bouncing off his back and head. The firing soon stopped as the guard was forced to reload. Mike began to sneak a peak around the table he was hiding behind as the rhythmic snap of a semi-automatic pistol sent him back for cover.

A naked blond landed next to him. She clutched her left midsection while crying and screaming, adding to the noise in the club. Several patrons were covered in blood, some were moving while others were not. When Debbie had said 'very hard' he never thought it would be this hard.

Debbie ran forward with her gun extended. The leader turned and caught her movement as he swung his weapon around to get a bead on her. He pulled the trigger early and the recoil sent the following bullets flying haphazardly around her. She fired in response and was thrown to the floor from the impact of a large man jumping on top of her small frame.

Her bullet grazed the leader's left arm and entered the right chest of the first guard, dropping him to his knees. Jim and Bill each put two more rounds into the first guard's chest before switching targets to the leader, who was already halfway out the front door.

Jim ran for the door, not to chase the leader but to make sure that he was not coming back in. He approached the door cautiously and was more than a bit relieved to see a large Cadillac leaving the parking lot in a hurry. It was moving too fast to see the plate but passed beneath a light, revealing its color, black. That man liked the color black.

Bill found Mike with one of his legs bleeding and his left hand pressed firmly against the gunshot wound of the naked blond. Mike's right hand had his gun at the ready. He glanced at Bill and nodded slowly.

"Did we get them all?" asked Mike.

"No, both guards are down but the leader got away," said Bill as he pulled the radio from his inside pocket and turned it on. He checked the frequency and pressed the transmit button before speaking. "Central, this is Dunne."

"Dunne, this is Central, go ahead."

"Spared Eagle, shots fired. One officer wounded, two suspects down, multiple bystanders wounded or dead. Need several ambulances and some backup."

"Acknowledged, help is on the way."

Bill looked up as Jim walked over and shook his head. The club was a mess. It looked like Beirut in the summer with blood and bodies everywhere. Tables were destroyed, people were crying and moaning, blood pooled in various spots, and somehow the music was still blaring. Half of the lights were shot out and as dim as the place was earlier it was difficult to see much of anything now.

"Long gone. A black Cadillac and I couldn't get the plate," said Jim loudly to be heard over the music. Then he yelled, "Can somebody turn that shit off?" Within seconds the music was gone and soon after that the lights came on. Then the moans of pain and suffering became more noticeable as the horror of a massacre revealed itself.

"Thank you," said Bill loudly into the air.

"What the hell did you say to them to piss them off, Mike?" asked

Jim.

"Not much. The shit hit the fan when the pictures hit the table," replied Mike as the girl screamed herself into unconsciousness. He holstered his gun and checked her pulse with his right hand. Her heart was still beating but the pulse was erratic. She was going into shock.

"I guess they recognized them," said Bill as he looked around for Debbie. "Where's Debbie?"

"Came in the back door," replied Mike as he looked in that direction.

Debbie tried to catch her breath as Sarge's hit knocked the wind out of her. Sarge placed his hands on the floor to both sides of her as he pushed himself up off of her body and relieved the pressure that caused her trouble with breathing. She coughed a few times and then smiled up at him.

"Thanks," said Debbie when she was able to. "I think."

"You okay?" asked Sarge.

"Yeah, but my ribs were still sore from being shot in the trauma plate a few days ago." The vest was something she could never do this job without, especially with the way her luck was going lately. She looked up from her chest into his eyes and instantly relaxed. "How about you?"

"Took one to the left shoulder. Been a while since I've taken a round. So, do you want to go out for coffee some morning?"

Debbie laughed softly. "I guess I have to now, since you took a round for me."

"Yup, there's a law for that somewhere," said Sarge with a smile as he stood slowly and tried to examine the wound. It was low on the shoulder and out of his view. He extended his right hand and helped Debbie to her feet.

Debbie scanned the room for hostiles and then holstered her weapon. Jim and Bill were making the rounds helping those that they could. Mike was laying on the floor holding the wound of a naked woman. He looked up from his task and winked in her direction. She smiled in return as sirens grew in the distance. Debbie was relieved to notice that someone had turned off the blaring music and put on the lights.

Several people exited from back rooms and began helping friends and patrons. Jim ran for the front door to greet those coming in so that they would know they were entering a secured environment.

Debbie ripped open the back of Sarge's shirt to look at the wound. There was quite a bit of blood and trying to stop it may have been more detrimental than leaving it alone.

"I can see the round lodged in your scapula. I think we'll just leave it there and let it plug whatever leaks it is currently stopping until the medics get here."

"Sounds reasonable, doc."

"The name is Debbie."

"It should be *pancake*."

"And yours should be *bulldozer*."

Sarge laughed as he looked down at the detective. She was rather short and small in comparison to his huge frame. But opposites attracted and he liked her strong will and determination. She had an air about her that reminded him of himself, and a confidence that he remembered having so very long ago. What was it about her? The warning chill up his spine was still there. Why was that still there? Hopefully dating would answer both questions.

The influx of emergency medical technicians and uniformed police officers quickly filled the destroyed club. The cleanup would take hours and then the paperwork would encompass many more. A medic began working on Sarge's shoulder as the wounded bouncer scanned the wrecked establishment.

"Shit," said Sarge as he spotted one of the wounded girls that he liked. He walked away from the annoyed EMT that reluctantly followed him. Debbie picked up the EMT's kit and followed them.

"Can't you sit still for one minute?" asked the EMT. "You'll make my job easier, but I'm sure you wouldn't want that, eh?"

"Sorry doc," replied Sarge as he sat down next to the girl on the floor. "I've lived through worse wounds." Her body was shaking in shock as Sarge picked up her hand and held it in his. He whispered some soothing words as one EMT worked carefully on stabilizing her vital signs while another patched her multiple gunshot wounds.

Debbie watched as the medic worked on Sarge's wound, he looked over his shoulder and winked at her and she smiled in return. It amazed her that he cared less about his own wound than that of another. He was someone special.

She had had a bad feeling about this night, but she did not think it would be this bad. The entire bar looked like a battlefront and, in a sad way, it was. The worst part about her bad feeling was that it was still there.

CHAPTER
13

PHILADELPHIA PA

The train was thirty minutes out of Philadelphia as Garrett watched the view outside pass by his window. The trees whipped by, quickly disappearing in the dim lights of nearby towns and cities. He scanned the car and saw several people with their eyes closed, trying to catch some sleep on the moving train. There was light talking around him and he listened absently to conversations as normal as any he had ever heard. Most people were concerned about all the work waiting for them in the morning. They would soon have other concerns, nothing they had any control over.

"Now," said the voice in Latin.

Garrett had almost forgotten about the earpiece, barely feeling its slight presence resting in his ear. He stood slowly and recovered his suitcase from the overhead rack before proceeding forward. A few cars ahead he found a restroom and went inside. Opening the suitcase he re-moved a small backpack packed firmly and fully. He checked the straps and put it on, cinching them tightly. There was another small bag inside the suitcase, which he opened quickly. It contained two boxes of 9mm ammunition and four full magazines. He put the boxes into his left pocket with the two empty magazines and the four fresh magazines went into his right pocket. He then checked the Uzi hanging under his left arm, which still had a full clip inserted.

He left the suitcase on the sink and entered the hallway, making his way forward at a steady pace. A few people passed by and hardly paid him any attention as they hurried along in their busy lives. Most never even acknowledged him while keeping their heads down, as some glanced at him and nodded slightly. Gone were the days of friendly banter among strangers. People kept to themselves, in their own little worlds, barely coming out to see the light of day.

Several cars from the engine, a steward wearing a white jacket and disinterest painted on his face exited one of the rooms and spotted him. For a few seconds he stared at Garrett while he pondered maintaining ignorance but then he approached, the decision made reluctantly.

"Excuse me sir, can I see your ticket and ID?"

"Sure thing," said Garrett as he swung the Uzi out from under his arm. He fired a controlled burst of three rounds at the man's center of mass to incapacitate, and it was more than enough to drop the surprised steward to the floor of the car. Garrett did not bother hiding the body, there was not enough time. He stepped over the unfortunate steward and continued down the hallway. He traversed the car and exited the final passenger car, making his way to the engineer station. Another worker appeared and Garrett sprayed a few rounds to riddle him with bullets, dropping him to the floor. The noise level increased and he barely heard the gun's action as the spent shells bounced around on the floor.

"Two more," said the voice in Latin.

Garrett kicked opened the final locked door on his third try, the restraining bolts damaged beyond repair. Both engineers looked back at him with surprise on their faces when they spotted the Uzi. He pulled the trigger and fired two controlled bursts of several rounds each, dropping both men to the floor in puddles of blood. Garrett ejected the half-spent magazine and then pulled a box of ammunition from his pocket. He refilled the clip from the box of ammo and reinserted it into the Uzi. He then filled the two empty clips, discarding one spent ammo box for the next. Once complete he pocketed the newly filled magazines and left the open box of ammo on the small table. Ammo was a thing to waste for this mission.

He briefly looked around the sparse control room and then examined the broken door. There would be no way he could secure this place to prevent someone from undoing his work. He would have to stay a bit longer than he had wanted to in order to assure this mission would be completed. He grunted silently at the thought of the coming challenge.

He eased the engine throttle forward slightly and the train responded by producing more power while slowly increasing speed. The GPS display on the instrument panel indicated where they were on the serpentine stretch of track extending from one side of the screen to the other. Garrett pressed the zoom button and examined the track until he found what he was looking for, a section which turned subtly. At their former speed it would have been no problem, but at full speed the train was sure to derail. He also had a bit of insurance waiting at that turn, just in case. Others on his team had recently placed a pound of explosives there that would be triggered as soon as he got within one hundred yards. It would blow a hole on the outside section of track so that the train would exit with ease.

Time ticked by rapidly and the train screeched around the current corner, centrifugal force causing him to readjust his stance. As soon as the train straightened out for the final time Garrett moved the throttle full forward. He then kicked the throttle from the side until it sheared off completely and bounced around on the floor.

"Two coming," said the voice in Latin.

Garrett ran to a corner of the room near the door and waited out of sight. Two stewards walked into the control room and approached the dead engineers. Garrett squeezed the trigger twice and both men dropped onto the other bodies. He slid along the wall and leaned forward to glance out the door. He was not quite sure why he checked, the voice would have told him if there had been any more coming. Maybe it was a habit from years ago finding its way to the surface. There was not enough time to ponder that line of thought.

The train continued accelerating and the vibrations increased making it difficult to stand still. Garrett ejected his current magazine and refilled it with bullets from the ammo box. It needed to be full and ready for the next part of this current mission. Everything was falling into place. Several missions wrapped together into one giant mission of precision. There was not much left to accomplish and his one long string of destruction was nearing an end.

A warning buzzer went off and Garrett found the silence button to turn off the annoying sound. The GPS display depicted the course and was flashing a warning that the current speed was too fast for this section of track. It indicated a slight turn that had a maximum speed far below that which they were traveling at. At his current speed the window of time to correct things was rapidly diminishing. Once it passed the point of no return, he waited a few seconds more before letting the Uzi fall by his left side. He exited the engineer room and made his way to the roof of the engine. The speed made it difficult for him to see very well in the high-speed wind and the darkness, but he knew the train was quickly approaching the turn. A flash in the near distance signaled the explosion although no sound could be heard above the din of the speeding train.

"Now," said the voice in Latin.

Garrett stood up as best he could and pulled the ripcord on his small reserve parachute. The pilot chute popped out and was instantly caught by the wind of the speeding train. After a very long few seconds the chute snapped fully open and jerked him forcefully backward, lifting him into the air. He did not gain that much altitude but it was more than enough to see the train jump the tracks and speed into the awaiting tree line. The rest of the cars followed in rapid succession and soon began stacking up as Garrett disappeared into a nearby clearing.

He hit the ground hard and quickly stripped the pack off his back. Garrett could easily hear the pained wrenching of metal that signified the death screams of a mechanical marvel. He began running at full speed through the clearing to the streetlights ahead. Timing was everything and he needed to be at that gas station in a hurry. The explosion echoed in the evening and reverberated off of the low-lying cloud layer. The yellowish-orange fireball caused the clouds to look as if it were sunset.

The pavement below his feet surprised him as he ran out in front of a small speeding car. The tires screeched as the driver locked up the brakes and jerked the car to the right to avoid the pedestrian. It was the wrong move to make and cost the middle-aged man his life as his car careened into a nearby tree. The impact sent the man's upper torso through the windshield while his legs were trapped between the dashboard and the seat. A section of glass nearly cut the man in half and he died a few seconds later in shocked pain.

Garrett did not pause and continued into the gas station parking lot to the bus that was waiting with its door open. A few shocked people watched in horror as a car crash occurred nearby. Several pointed at the man that caused the wreck as he approached their bus. A few people opened their cell phones to call 9-1-1 while others stared in silence, not believing their eyes.

The door was still open when Garrett arrived. The stunned bus driver turned from the wreck outside to look at the man at the foot of the steps. He opened his mouth to speak but was silenced when a burst of several 9mm rounds entered his skull and body. Garrett ran up the steps and pulled the man from behind the wheel, throwing him to the floor next to him. Screams of surprise and shock filled the bus as Garrett sat down in the driver's seat and jammed the bus into gear. As the bus exited the gas station parking lot, he watched several people run to the small car.

A few people on the bus stood and were making their way forward but Garrett saw them approach in the mirror. He twisted his body and held the Uzi so he could fire straight down the walkway. He flipped the selector to full auto and sprayed bullets in their direction. Two men dropped to the floor as several of the other passengers were hit by stray rounds. Garrett jerked the steering wheel to the right so he would stay on the road as he ejected the spent magazine onto the floor. He held the steering wheel steady with his left knee as he inserted a full clip from his right pocket into the Uzi. He accelerated the bus and passed the speed limit as he held the gun upside down over his shoulder to dump another clip into the screaming passengers behind him.

A police cruiser that was hiding in the trees waiting for speeders caught the bus on radar doing twenty miles per hour over the speed limit. He saw the flashes of light and thought nothing of it as the bus rocketed past his position. He flipped on his lights and pulled behind the bus while accelerating for pursuit.

Garrett ejected another spent magazine and reloaded with his last full clip as the screaming increased. Various pleas and begging assault-ed his senses as he noticed the flashing cruiser lights growing behind him. He switched to single-fire mode and turned around to look at the passengers, selectively shooting those that remained alive. Then he popped the belt clasp and tossed the empty Uzi to the floor, grabbing the body of the dead bus driver. He pulled the man closer and jammed his corpse against the accelerator pedal. Garrett lined the bus up with a row of people waiting at a small theater and jumped out of the still open door. He hit the ground off balance and rolled several yards before slamming against a parked car, setting off its alarm.

"Oops," said Garrett as he reflexively clutched his left arm. He muted the shaft of pain shooting through his mind to just a dull buzz as he shook his head. Garrett stood and began running awkwardly between the closest buildings, hopefully before anyone saw him. The pain diminished as his mind succeeded in suppressing it.

"Move, quickly," said the voice in Latin.

"Which way?" asked Garrett as the screams of a panicked crowd of people were silenced by a loud crash, followed by the piercing shriek of a siren from the pursuing police cruiser.

"Left, thirty degrees. Four streets over."

Garrett exited the alley and modified his course slightly. Walking as best he could while clutching his left arm, he soon found himself four streets over and saw the building with the numbers he recognized from some time ago. He stopped and crouched in the alley as he carefully watched the area around the apartment building. The building was old and worn down and gave low-income housing a good name. The bricks showed signs of wear even in the dim glow of the streetlights. It stood four stories tall and all the windows were intact. Several plants were displayed on windowsills, confirming that people did actually live here. The only abnormal activity was a few of the upper windows opening to see where the commotion was coming from as sirens polluted the once silent evening.

Garrett clutched his left arm and cautiously slid his left hand into his jacket pocket as he stood. He waited a few more seconds and saw no movement or anyone not completely entranced by the recent bus crash. He crossed the street in the shadows with his teeth gritted as the pain from his damaged arm shouted for acknowledgment. He entered the apartment complex and found the room he was looking for on the second floor. The door was not locked and he entered after pausing to see if anyone in the small hallway was watching. The kitchen light was already on and he closed the door, locking it behind himself as he sighed slightly in relief. It was another very active night in his life completed and he was tired, but now it was time for him to take care of his broken arm.

The apartment was very small with only two real rooms, the bath-room and the living area. The living area had a bed and the kitchen was in a niche along the left wall, butted up against the small bathroom. A poor excuse for a table and chair occupied a space with barely enough room to open the refrigerator door. A small cardboard box containing several bananas and apples was placed in the center of the table. Garrett emptied the box on the bed and pulled the tape off the bottom of it. He opened the box up and folded it into a triangular section about four inches on each side and two feet long. He carefully laid his broken arm into it and closed the triangle off, managing to wrap the tape around it. The tape barely had enough stick left to it so he did the best he could with tying it closed. He then grabbed hold of an old metal radiator with his left hand and jerked backward. A sharp pain shot up his arm and he gritted his teeth as his broken bones aligned themselves.

"Ah, much better," said to himself through gritted teeth, "I think."

Garrett opened the refrigerator and removed a gallon jug of water, which was the only thing inside. He pulled the safety plastic off the cap and opened it, taking a long pull that emptied a fourth of its contents into his awaiting mouth. He returned it to the fridge and placed the fruit one by one onto the table to clear the bed. Peeling a banana one-handed was an interesting feat but he soon consumed that as fast as he had the water, tossing the remaining peel into the sink. He then ate one of the apples, bouncing the core off the refrigerator door and into the sink. He turned off the sole kitchen light and laid out on the covers of the bed and fell asleep instantly. It had been a long day, a very long day, and now he needed to take some time to rest and heal.

CHAPTER
14

Debbie entered the hospital carrying a tray with three cups of coffee secured in it. She knew from experience that the hospital's coffee needed a lot of help and she did not want to subject her friends to any unnecessary pain. It was bad enough that they had to eat the food, but that would be a lot more difficult to sneak in. She knew the floor they were on and entered the awaiting and recently vacated elevator. She pressed number three and waited patiently. Her chest was still sore from being shot by a psychopath and then later run over by an overprotective bouncer named Sarge. Her breathing was still somewhat labored, but that was a lot better than the other alternative. Who could have known where the bullet that Sarge took would have went had he not been there.

She ran the entire confrontation through her memory and analyzed every single aspect. What had they gained last night? The only thing that came to mind was body count. Several innocent bystanders had died or been injured in the firefight. One detective, her partner, was out of action for a couple of weeks. Loose ends? Two dead leads in a case that was going nowhere fast. The leader got away but they had a good description of him, and maybe even a name. One of the girls that they interviewed after the mess knew him as Sergei. She seemed to think he was Polish or maybe Russian. Seeing that he always ordered the most expensive vodka when he was there, Debbie was leaning toward the latter of the two. But there was no real way to tell yet since anybody could enjoy drinking expensive vodka. Was that enough information to track him down? It had to be. At least she hoped as much.

The door opened and Debbie exited the elevator, taking a right down the hallway. Several interns or students were being led by a nurse with the look of frustration and annoyance as plain as day written on her face. The nurse glanced briefly at her before turning the corner with her parade close behind. Debbie turned a corner in the opposite direction and watched the room numbers go by. She knew both of their room numbers and they were not very far from each other. Mike's room was first on her list to stop at and for some reason that she did not quite understand she dreaded this meeting.

"Room service," said Debbie as she entered Mike's room. Another woman looked up from the side of the bed and examined her with an almost contemptuous gaze. Debbie's first reaction was one of relief. The blond girl was in her mid-twenties and may have been a model with that perfect shapely body screaming out to be noticed by anyone with eyes. She was well-dressed besides, and her short blond hair gave her a wild look that made her appear sexy and adventurous.

"Hey partner," said Mike as he looked away from the blond girl and at Debbie. Debbie looked as lovely to him as usual and more tired than she normally did.

"You okay?" asked Debbie carefully.

"Oh yeah, doc says I'll be out of here tomorrow. The bullet went clean through, missing all the important stuff."

Debbie opened her mouth to make a comment but hesitated and

then closed it. Then she opened it again but could not find the right words, so she closed it again and sighed. She grabbed a cup of coffee from the tray and handed it to him. "I brought you some real coffee."

"Thanks," said Mike with a smile. He took a sip and nodded with a sigh. "Much better."

"Would you like a cup?" asked Debbie of the blond.

"No," replied the girl with a touch of anger.

"We can share," said Mike quickly, oblivious to the tense atmosphere between the two women. He had coffee now, and nothing else mattered.

"What's your problem?" asked Debbie while looking into the girl's blue eyes. Two could play the anger game and Debbie had had about enough of this crap. The girl was young and beautiful and had a huge chip on her shoulder about something and Debbie wanted to knock it off. Being reserved all the time meant being quiet and she was done with that. Debbie was tired of caring, tired of always being the good little girl never hurting anyone's feelings, tired of having to be the strong-willed one, and just plain tired.

"You almost got him killed!" the girl nearly yelled out as she clenched her fists and began shaking with anger. "Get out of here, leave us alone."

Debbie turned and headed for the door. She opened it quickly and was halfway out when she heard Mike calling to her. She ignored him and the belligerent girl as the door shut softly behind her. Part of her wanted to cry. Did she almost get Mike killed? Did she almost get herself killed? Did she get all those other people killed or wounded in her blind pursuit of a killer or killers? Was there any way she could have known that things would have gone down as badly as they had? It could have been worse. It could have been a lot worse. Was that any kind of consolation? She had too many questions without answers. The more she thought about it the more she did not want to.

She stopped outside of the next door and sighed heavily while looking at the tray with two cups of coffee in her hands. She really hoped things went better in this room. Part of her expected the worst. The other part hoped for the better. Debbie was so tired of everything being out of control in her life she almost screamed out in protest. She opened the door slowly and peered into the room, the muscles in her legs tightening in anticipation of running away. The near bed was empty but the bed by the window was occupied.

"Hey, Pancake," said Sarge with a huge smile on his face and his left arm in a sling. He was sitting up in his bed watching the news on the television while an empty tray table sat beside him.

"Hi Kurt."

"You can call me Sarge, you know."

"I know, but I like Kurt better."

Kurt nodded, thinking of how the strippers he worked with always wanted to hide behind a name. Did he still need to hide? Maybe. Did he need to hide from her? "So, how are you?"

"I'm," started Debbie with a pause, "well, let's just say that I'm having an interesting day so far."

"Oh, that good? Looks like you just got into a fight with emotions and lost." Kurt wiggled aside and patted the empty area next to him. "Here, have a seat."

"I brought you some coffee," replied Debbie while sitting down on the bed, roughly facing him. She popped the top off and handed him the cup. His eyes lit up as he took a strong sniff of the wonderfully dark liquid.

"Ah," said Kurt as he took another long sniff. "Coffee that doesn't smell like paint thinner. Thank you, Debbie." He took a small sip and smiled with a satisfied sigh.

"Kurt, how's your shoulder?"

"Feels a bit sore but the doc says it's fine. My bone has a spider-web-like fracture in it now but that was about it. Wanna see the scar?" finished Kurt in excitement.

Debbie laughed in response and shook her head, "I saw the hole, remember?"

"Oh yeah, that's right."

She popped off the top of her cup and took a slow sip of the hot liquid. Her thoughts drifted to the angry girl and Mike. She did not want to spend her day thinking about them or worrying about how she fit into that puzzle. She had work to do and a case to try and solve. Once again duty called.

"Are you angry?" asked Kurt.

"More confused than angry. I saw my partner a few minutes ago and there was a girl in his room that I locked horns with. She outright hates me, for some odd reason. I never met her before. It felt like I was intruding."

"The only girl in my room is you, so there's none of that going on here."

"I half expected to walk into a room full of strippers," said Debbie as she looked at him out of the corner of her right eye. She took another sip of coffee while waiting for some kind of response.

Kurt sighed and nodded slowly. "Not with me. They may come and visit, but after the mess last night most will probably go and work somewhere else. Somewhere safer. Somewhere three states away. I only work there because the money is good and I don't have any real skills, except killing people. I can't do that legally anymore."

"Why did you leave the Marines?" asked Debbie as she turned to look directly into his brilliant blue eyes. They were so soft and peaceful that she could have stared into them for hours without a care in the world.

"Got shot up pretty badly in Desert Storm," replied Kurt as he leaned back against the pillow. He grunted slightly as the pain in his left shoulder increased with the pressure. "An Iraqi tank round hit my buddy and I was showered with shrapnel and body parts. I lost my left kneecap and several of my internal organs were badly torn open, I almost died. I can still feel the weak points inside me whenever I work out. I was in eleven years at that point, but I couldn't pass the physical requirements to requalify. Because of my service record they let me stay in for another year until I came up for reenlistment. Then it was time for me to get out."

Debbie was not sure what to say or how to respond so she nodded and took another sip of coffee. They sat silently for several minutes and listened to the newscaster babbling in the background. Another tragedy had occurred when a large passenger train wrecked just outside of the city killing hundreds of people. Then within a mile of the wreck a bus driver went psycho and killed his passengers before crashing into a crowd of people standing outside of a movie theater. She wondered what was becoming of the world.

"I miss it," said Kurt with a sigh. "I would've been a lifer, for sure."

Debbie finished her coffee and put it on the tray near his bed. After a reluctant pause she rubbed his right knee with her right hand and slowly stood up. "I need to get going. I have a case to solve."

"Be safe and watch your back. Those guys are bastards."

She nodded as she pulled a business card out of her pocket along with a pen. She quickly wrote a number on the back of it and handed it to him. "My work number is on the front and my home number is on the back. Call me," said Debbie with a smile. She leaned in and kissed him on the right cheek before turning to leave.

"Count on it."

"I'll stop by later and say hi," said Debbie as she opened the door. She turned and looked at the strong-willed man lying in bed with his left arm in a sling. Their eyes locked and several seconds of silence passed before she winked and exited the room.

Mike's room was to the left and she stood in the hallway a few seconds as she pondered that puzzle. Avoidance was her first thought so she went right and found a stairwell to descend. It was a long slow walk to the ground floor and she struggled to clear the confrontation from her mind. She still had work to do and there was no time to dwell on things she not only did not understand but could not relate to. Mike was a good guy and a good partner but who was that girl? Debbie had no feelings for Mike and did not want any. It was purely a working relationship and needed to stay that way, no matter how much she felt that part missing from her life. But who was that girl? Why did she hate her so much? It just did not make sense, and Mike did not have the decency to introduce them.

Then there was Kurt. A man so different from her usual tastes. He looked like a bodybuilder or wrestler or maybe both wrapped up in one. Something about his eyes just cried out for her, almost as if in pain? That made no sense to her. She needed somebody to share life with but that someone needed to understand her. She loved her dangerous job and that always seemed to come first, and most men could not deal with that, or maybe did not want to try. Maybe they were so insecure with themselves that they felt they needed to control her, and that was never going to happen. She needed a strong man, someone mentally strong and self-assured. Debbie saw that particular something in Kurt, and it worried and excited her. She really did hope he would call and she would definitely stop by to see him tonight as well. Was there something there? It was worth finding out. She needed to find out.

The door to the outside world opened and Debbie stepped into the broken sunlight. The low-lying cloud layer was still there, reluctant to burn off completely, but streams of sunlight made their way through. It was a brisk day and she paused for a moment to take a deep breath, which caused the shooting pain to radiate from her still-sore chest.

She did not notice the car less than a block away with two men inside of it. They watched her with interest through binoculars until she disappeared around the corner and out of their sight. The car started and turned down the street behind her.

CHAPTER
15

PHILADELPHIA PA

G arrett awoke suddenly and stared at the cardboard wrapped around his left arm. He concentrated on it for a minute before he grabbed the end by his hand and slid his arm out slowly. The arm was sore as he flexed his left hand into a fist. He moved his wrist and then moved his arm around in circles as he felt for evidence of the breaks with his right hand, but found none. The only indications were the overly sore portions, still very tender but repaired enough that he had a full range of motion with it. It would most likely be sore for a few days but he could still function while favoring his right arm.

He grabbed a banana from the table and peeled it, then stuffed the soft part into his awaiting mouth as he opened the refrigerator door. The banana did not last long and the peel joined the other one in the sink as he took the gallon of water out and opened it, pouring another quart into his mouth. He then ate another apple as he looked around at the accommodations. There was not much of anything else in this small apartment, except a few pieces of furniture and a bathroom. He stripped quickly and entered the shower that he had craved for days. There was no hot water, which did not surprise him, but he did not appear to notice the difference as he took the cake of soap and lathered up. He cleaned the grime from his skin and the salt water from his matted and sticky hair. The cold water felt refreshing to him and awakened him even further. It was a quick shower, lasting less than five minutes, but it was more than enough. He dried off and stared at his very soiled clothing on the floor. He knew it smelled but had no choice, he had to wear it for there was nothing else available. The apartment was not part of the plan, just something he knew of and needed for a brief recovery.

Garrett put the earpiece in his left ear and waited as he looked at himself in the mirror. His hair was clean now and he could use a shave but that would have to wait. After a minute of nothingness he pulled his pants on and then his shirt. The fishy smell of the Chesapeake Bay via the Atlantic Ocean was still there despite changing his clothes at the train station. But that might be a good thing with where he was going. He sat on the side of the bathtub and pulled his socks and then sneakers on. His clothes could be the rattiest pieces of garbage on the planet as long as he had a good pair of shoes. That was one rule he had to live by in his line of work. It was the only thing he asked of his boss, the only thing he really wanted.

His first order of business was to procure a weapon. He had up to seven days left to complete the contract in this city before he needed to disappear for a while. The exact amount of time was flexible and unknown, events had yet to occur. Every year that technology advanced it made things more and more difficult for him to fade away after a job. The constabulary might eventually catch up to him. Soon he would outlive his usefulness, at least in this country.

Garrett put his jacket on and exited the apartment, making his way quickly to the bottom floor. Once out on the street he went north and had no urge to check out his handiwork from last night. The bus accident was most likely crawling with people that would be looking for him and he did not want to help them out. He ignored everyone as he found that everyone was ignoring him. Garrett looked like a street bum, and definitely smelled like one, so he fit in quite well. Most people put as much distance from him as they could while they walked down the street.

"Hey buddy, over here," said a whispered voice from the alley to his right.

Garrett stopped and looked at the man by the alley entrance. He was young, maybe early twenties from his face. He stood up straight and had an air of confidence about him that belied his age. This was a man that lived on the streets and fed from them. Fed from the people, fed from the environment, and fed from society as a whole. He was not just a street thug, he owned a part of the street. Normally Garrett would ignore this kind of challenge but he needed a weapon and the odds were really good that this kid had one.

"Yes," said the voice in Latin in his earpiece.

Garrett cautiously entered the alley. He slumped his shoulders as a bum would, just trying to go unnoticed in this massive world. Ignored and left alone. Living by the adage, 'act like a victim and be a victim', he approached the man slowly. "Yes?" asked Garrett as he stood five feet from the man and watched him closely.

"What are you doing here? This area is mine and I don't know you."

"Just passing through," said Garrett as he watched the man's feet.

"Well, go around."

"Can't," replied Garrett. He hoped this was enough of a challenge to this man's authority.

"You stupid bum," said the young man as he came away from the wall and grabbed Garrett's coat by the neck. He pulled Garrett deeper into the alley and Garrett let him. Once they were almost forty feet from the street the man threw Garrett up against the wall and reached into his own jacket.

Garrett did not wait, he charged the man. The shocked expression on the young man's face was quickly marred as Garrett punched him in the nose. That was all it took, the man fell to the pavement and was dead before he hit the ground. His face had been caved in with the look of shock permanently etched on what remained.

Garrett eyed the blood on his right knuckles and wiped it off on his shirt. He removed his old clothes and tossed them into a nearby dumpster. Then he undressed the young man, whose clothes were clean and unbloodied. The man had a large .45 caliber handgun under his arm and Garrett's eyes lit up. It was his weapon of choice whenever he actually had a choice.

Once he was dressed, Garrett looked at the dead man lying nearly naked in the alleyway. It was his street alright, it was also his final resting place. His rats would be having a feast very soon unless someone found him first and removed him. But that was not Garrett's concern. Scum like that reaped what they sowed and it was harvest time. He had things to do and a long way to walk before the end of this day.

Garrett reached into the back pocket of his new pants and removed the man's wallet. He extracted the large wad of money from it and pocketed the bills before tossing the wallet onto the body. Other scavengers would take whatever else they could find before the police could arrive. Nothing left behind would remain unmolested for very long.

He exited the alleyway carefully and checked for anyone that may have been watching. Nobody seemed to care or notice the recent events. It was a silent and quick death and in any city it should have gone unnoticed. Or if noticed there was still the possibility that it would be ignored. Most citizens did not want to be a part of anything for fear that the criminals would take their frustrations out on them.

Garrett entered the street in his last direction and moved a little more confidently and easily. No longer needing to act like a smelly bum, he stood tall and made better time. There was no place that he really needed to be yet so he kept walking and watching and remained ready for immediate action, if necessary. It was now time for his boss to do his thing.

CHAPTER
16

D ebbie parked in front of the alley where the three bodies were found and exited her car. She looked up at the buildings around the alley for any vantage points where someone may have seen people enter or exit the alley. The two buildings were both four stories tall and had numerous emergency escape routes and landings, but would anyone admit they saw anything? In the case of two dead strippers and a third woman whose purpose still remained a mystery, the possibility of anyone caring were slim to none.

She entered the alley and walked slowly while taking in the surrounding scenery. Various trash cans and boxes lined the right side of the small alley, allowing more than enough room for a vehicle to enter. She doubted that a trash truck could fit in the small confines at this end but should have enough room using the other entrance. Her nose scrunched up as the vile smells assaulted her senses. She could not imagine this place in the heat of summer as the sun baked the stench right out of the garbage. How bums could live in that kind of setting completely boggled her mind.

The alley went straight ahead and came out at the next block while a portion turned to the left and became a dead end twenty-five feet in. Around the corner was where the three girls met their fate with the executioner. Debbie slowed and paused as she examined the wall to her left. Something caught her attention in one of the bricks on the wall. A recent chip of cement between the bricks was missing and there was something inside the open space. She removed a plastic bag and a pair of tweezers she kept in her left breast pocket. She worked the projectile out and examined it carefully. It was a squashed .22 caliber round that had dried blood and a possible hair still attached to it. One of the girls took a round to the head and the bullet had exited her left eye socket. The alley had been searched for hours to find that missing piece of evidence but with no luck, until now.

Debbie dropped the bullet into the plastic bag and sealed it closed. Then she put the tweezers and the bag into her pocket as she continued her search of the area. If she could find one clue that quickly what others would she find? *Maybe this case does have a solution*, thought Debbie as she crouched down in a corner to examine some refuse.

"Find anything?" asked a deep and heavily accented male voice from behind her.

Debbie turned quickly and reached for the gun under her jacket. A quick count of all the legs she saw made her heart rate soar through the roof, accentuating the sore spot in her chest that signified a previous mistake.

"Don't bother, lady, you'd be dead before you could get it out of your holster."

Debbie raised both hands and stood up slowly as she assessed the six men standing before her. Not all of them were tall but most had dark hair and several sported scars on their faces. One of them she recognized immediately as Sergei. He was the only one not holding a weapon while the other five men held MAC-11s, all pointed at her.

What troubled her the most was that this trip was just supposed to be a routine check of a past crime scene. She did not think that she would have needed backup for this. She was wrong on a level she could not imagine. She was not sure what can of worms she opened but it was a big one, with more slime than she ever cared to dream about.

"What do you want?" asked Debbie as she tried to find a way out of the alley. Both visible doors had deadbolts on them and were most definitely secured from within as well. With all six men in front of her there was no way she could get out of this alive, unless they wanted her to, which she doubted. This would not be an execution, it would be a slaughter.

"Revenge," said Sergei evenly as he approached her. His men walked forward with him and three stopped halfway there while two of them walked alongside him. All of their eyes were focused on her, in case she tried something, which would have been the dumbest thing she could ever do.

"For what?"

"Two of my very good friends at *The Spared Eagle*." Sergei grabbed Debbie by the hair at the back of her head with his right hand and jerked it backward causing her to grunt with the pain. He pulled the weapon out of her shoulder holster and tossed it into a nearby trash can, the ring of metal hitting metal echoing briefly. Sergei then punched her in the stomach as hard as he could and she folded over while he released her hair. Then he grabbed the hair at the top of her head with his right hand and punched her with his left in her left cheek. She fell to the ground as her lip split open and bled.

"You not so tough," said Sergei with a slight chuckle as he released his grip on her hair. "Maybe me and my friends use you first."

"Like the prostitutes you killed in this alley?" asked Debbie feebly as the blood flowed from her mouth. It had a metallic taste that was warm and drops of blood fell from her chin to the ground. She spat out a bunch of blood onto Sergei's shoe and he backed up a step.

"Dirty whores! All women are dirty whores to be used and discarded when done."

"Why did you kill them?" asked Debbie, who realized her fate would soon mirror theirs. The other men in the alley tensed, adjusting their grips on the weapons as the time to use them rapidly approached.

"I am done with you so why not ask them yourself," said Sergei with a sick and rather twisted smile. He grabbed a handful of her hair as he reached for the .22 caliber revolver in the holster at his side.

CHAPTER
17

PHILADELPHIA PA

"A lley, left, hurry," said the voice rapidly in Latin.

Garrett turned in surprise and began running as fast as he could make his legs move. It had been a long time since he had heard such urgency in his boss' voice. He pulled the .45 from his shoulder holster with his right hand and racked the slide with his left, putting a round in the chamber. He flipped on the safety and tucked the weapon behind his belt, concealing it with his jacket as he approached a road with another alley straight ahead.

"Across, in the alcove," said his boss, the urgency more evident.

Garrett leaped onto the hood of a slowly passing car and shocked the driver into stopping. He bounded into the next alley and continued in wonderment at what lie ahead. Several trash cans and boxes lined the left wall as a break in the right wall approached. By instinct he slowed and approached the turn cautiously. As the opening arrived he saw several men with machine guns pointed at a woman on the ground with an unarmed man standing over her. The unarmed man's right fist held her by a handful of hair and his left hand was under his jacket, most likely reaching for a pistol.

"Save her," said the voice in Latin.

Garrett took three steps forward and purposefully kicked a can and all the men turned around quickly and targeted him. By the looks on most of their faces they were well-trained and waited for their leader to say something. Garrett spent a fraction of a second looking at each of the men before his highly-trained brain took over. He categorized and sorted each one and placed them into a target priority hierarchy, with the most likely threats to react at the top of the list.

"Just keep going or you will join her," yelled the man in English. He appeared to be the leader, or at least the one in charge of the others. His position on the threat list was number five, whereas the closest man to Garrett held the number six rating.

Garrett glanced at the girl on her knees and her eyes begged for his help. She knew she was going to die and she was scared. Then Garrett carefully eyed the unarmed man grasping her hair and shrugged. "Not my problem," said Garrett evenly as he turned around to head back in the direction he had come from. He eased the pistol out of his belt and clicked off the safety as he casually walked away.

"Don't screw with the Russian mafia, asshole," said another man in Russian as he raised his weapon to fire.

Garrett yelled out in perfectly fluent Russian, "Hell is waiting for you, there are reservations for six." He spun and crouched while firing six rounds as rapidly as he could pull the trigger. He went down his targeting list in less time than it took to create it. Six very loud reports from his .45 caliber weapon echoed in the alleyway as each projectile impacted a Russian mafia member. The bodies dropped like dominoes to the pavement and Garrett stood while holstering his weapon in one fluid motion.

He approached the woman and held out his left hand for her to take. She took it apprehensively as she looked deeply into his eyes, and saw nothingness.

"Who are you?" she asked feebly as her legs failed to give her a stable platform to stand on. She dropped to one knee while continuing to watch the strange man in front of her.

"No one. I was just passing by and thought I would help a lady in distress," replied Garrett. "Who are you?"

"Debbie Mason. Philly homicide."

"You were almost a corpse," said Garrett. He carefully grabbed her upper arm and nearly carried her as he led her away from the alley polluted with more dead bodies.

Debbie looked down at the six dead men as she passed them, not believing what had just occurred in front of her. The left side of her face hurt badly and she was certain she would have a black eye by noon. Her vest absorbed some of the punch to the stomach and for that she was grateful. That would surely have caused the pain in her chest to resurface. She now knew how helpless all of the housewives on those domestic calls she had been to in the past had felt.

As they exited the alley Garrett spotted a coffee shop to his left. He helped her to the door and they entered as several people watched them with interest and began whispering to each other. Garrett gently sat her down at a table near the front window and handed her some napkins for the blood on her lip.

"Can I get you anything?" asked a young waitress as the cold look in Garrett's eyes made her knees quiver.

"Two coffees please," replied Garrett.

"Yes sir," replied the girl as she left their table rapidly while the other patrons went back to their own little worlds.

"What did that guy say to you?" asked Debbie once the waitress had left.

"Something about not screwing with the Russian mafia," replied Garrett as he watched the people moving around outside. The activity was normal despite the recent gunfire. That was one of the pluses about working in a big city. The police usually dragged their feet a bit on calls reporting shots fired. It was not a wise thing to walk into someone else's gunfight.

"You speak Russian?"

"Occasionally," replied Garrett with a shrug.

"What was your response?"

"Nothing worth mentioning."

"Did you have to kill them?" asked Debbie in a whisper.

"They were dead inside, what was the difference?" answered Garrett as he pulled some money from his pocket and put it on the table. The waitress arrived and placed a cup in front of each of them. Then she filled them with coffee and took the money, quickly leaving the table.

"Dead inside?" asked Debbie as she stared at the full cup in front of her. It was black and the twisting tendrils of steam mesmerized her. She wanted to look at the man but just could not bring herself to look into his eyes again. Just the thought of those vacant eyes made a shiver run down her spine.

"The only thing they brought to this world was grief. The world is a better place without them," said Garrett as he opened a creamer and dumped it into her coffee. He did the same for his own and stirred both with a spoon.

"You don't seem very phased by what you did. Are you a vigilante?"

Garrett took a sip of his coffee and nodded slowly. "In a way, I guess I would be perceived as such."

"You're a good shot," said Debbie as she chanced a sip of her coffee. It was hot and her bloodied lip hurt like hell, and the liquid only managed to send more pain to her already sore and throbbing head.

"I never miss."

"Have you killed many people?"

"Yes."

"How many?" she asked after a slight pause, not really sure she wanted to know the answer.

"Hundreds of thousands, or so," replied Garrett as he cupped his earpiece so he could hear with all the background noise in the coffee shop.

Debbie stammered in shock, unsure of how to respond to him except with her continued silence. She raised her eyes and looked at the man sitting in front of her. There was absolutely no remorse in him, in his eyes, or in his mannerisms. The recent six murders mattered not a bit to him. Whether casually sipping a cup of coffee or blowing away the Russian mafia, his demeanor would remain the same. Calm, cool, and collected. She was positive that he could easily lie his way through a lie detector without batting an eye. This man was a killing machine.

Garrett finished his coffee and stood. "Your friends are coming. I've got to go."

"Thank you," said Debbie as she managed to look him in the eyes again and Garrett smiled in response. The smile appeared genuine and instantly sent a wave of calm assurance throughout her body.

"You're welcome."

"How can I reach you?"

Garrett produced a business card from his jacket pocket and handed it to her before he headed for the exit. She scanned it quickly and noticed the phone number as he was halfway out the door.

"What area code?" she asked as she turned her head toward him.

"It's local," replied Garrett. He turned left and disappeared as sirens increased in the distance.

Debbie sipped her coffee and winced as several cruisers pulled up and stopped in front of the alley. Officers swarmed down the alley with weapons drawn as the coffee shop patrons watched in wonderment. She examined the card and immediately noticed the plainness of it. It was plain white and oddly enough it appeared as if it had been run through a washing machine and air dried. It had only four lines of text on it;

Garrett Carmichael, CAD Specialist, SM Division, and a phone number without an area code. She slipped it into her pocket as she finished her coffee.

The alleyway looked different this time as she entered it after flashing her badge for the officers standing at the opening. Her face hurt and her lip felt like a balloon. She knew she looked like hell, but she was alive, thanks to a mysterious man. Part of her wanted to detain him for questioning but it was her life that he had saved by risking his own. Did he actually risk his life? She seriously doubted it. The entire affair did not seem to cause him any distress whatsoever, no remorse, and that unnerved her. Maybe he was a marine but working the only way he knew how, killing people. Her thoughts drifted to Kurt. Would he too act like this man? Was this one possible future for him?

"Debbie!" yelled Bill as he ran to her and lifted up her chin. "What the hell kind of bus hit you?"

"A bus named Sergei," replied Debbie as she tried to push him out of the way. He would not budge as Jim came to his side.

"You're a mess," said Jim while shaking his head. "Who did this to you?"

"Your favorite Russian corpse," replied Debbie while pointing to the body without a weapon in its hand. She scanned the bodies from where she was standing and noted that all six men had a single hole in their forehead and a look of shock on their faces. That mysterious man was either very lucky or an exceptional marksman.

"Hey, yeah, holy shit, it is," said Jim in surprise. "I didn't even recognize that asshole."

"Not a single shot fired from them either. All of their guns were on full auto and had the safeties off with a round in the chamber, but not one was fired. The guys that took them down were really good and had the jump on them too," said Bill as he glanced around, scanning the tops of buildings for snipers.

"Just one guy," said Debbie as she walked over to the trash can to recover her sidearm. She checked the clip and the round in the chamber before returning it to her holster.

"Bullshit," shot Bill in response. "Nobody is that good. It would've taken six men firing in sync in order to drop them before they could even reflexively squeeze off some rounds. It's just not possible for one guy to do this."

"I saw it happen while I was kneeling over there getting the shit beat out of me."

"Maybe you imagined it."

"Nope, had coffee with the guy afterward. One very cool customer. A pro." Debbie examined the blood on the ground where she had spat on Sergei's shoe after her lip was split open. She would have died right at that very spot just a few seconds later. Dead just like the three strippers with a .22 caliber round in the back of her head. She probably should have died right there.

"But why?" asked Jim as he knelt near the dead leader of this band of men.

"I don't know. I'm alive, so I wonder if I should even care what his motive for saving me was."

Bill looked at Debbie and watched her stare at the dead leader. He had seen men crack up before, especially after a near death experience, and knew the signs that she was getting ready to lose it. He came up behind her and pulled her away from the grisly scene. She did not resist as he walked her out of the alley and had her sit down on the hood of one of the nearby patrol cars.

"You okay?" he asked while holding her head up to look into her eyes. Her face was a bloody and bruised mess.

"Yes," replied Debbie as she stared off into the distance at absolutely nothing. "No."

"I'm sending you to the hospital," said Bill while motioning for the nearest EMT. "We'll finish up here while you get some rest."

"Okay," replied Debbie as the EMT began examining her. He

cleaned up her cut lip and then applied a salve to lessen the pain in the bruise around her eye.

"Come with me," said the EMT as he helped her to the awaiting ambulance. She was the only one here requiring his services and the fleet of coroner vehicles nearby would handle the rest. He helped her into the back of the ambulance and had her lie down as he began checking her vitals. The driver did not wait for the word to go, as soon as the door slammed shut he began moving.

Garrett watched the scene from a distance. He never stuck around after his work was complete to see what happened, it never interested him nor did it usually matter. He was safer as far from the incident as possible but Debbie interested him. He knew he would meet her again, otherwise things would not have played out as they had. For the first time in his life he was curious, and he did not like it one bit.

CHAPTER
18

PHILADELPHIA PA

It was the longest night of her life, as much as she could remember of it. Her brief trip to the hospital told her nothing new and then Jim was kind enough to check on her and take her home. He had another detective pick up her vehicle and leave it at her apartment. Debbie really felt like she was in a family with her department. They would all bend over backward to help each other out when the chips were down.

She lay in bed staring at the ceiling as the television flickered in the darkness. It was well past midnight and the same news broadcast was replayed ad nauseam. The current conspiracy theory followed a terrorist group's trail across the East Coast. It began at thirty-five thousand feet over the Atlantic as a jet liner disappeared from radar and went into the drink. Then a luxury cruise ship met a similar fate, sitting irrecoverably at the bottom of the ocean. Then a massive supertanker full of oil slams into a city waking up for the early morning commute.

Next comes a small lapse in so-called accidents from Norfolk to

Philadelphia. But one sporadic event, a bizarre vehicle redecoration in some small town in Virginia, between Norfolk and Petersburg, might possibly tie it all together. When a train, from Petersburg, derails outside of Philadelphia the link between accidents is quickly established and a path is drawn. But witnesses at the scene of the redecoration say that it was only one man. He was of average size, average build, and all around average looking. It was so nondescript that all investigating agencies threw it into the 'good luck solving this one' pile. The man had no distinctive features or marks that would single him out. That matched millions of people. Throw in not even a single fingerprint and it was the icing on the proverbial cake. To top it all off, in this digital age, not a single person caught the redecoration on video.

The red pickup truck the shooter was using was recovered in Texas. The man found driving it wanted to leave Virginia in a hurry and did not want to wait for a bus. He said he found the keys left in it, which the arresting officers found in the man's possession, and just took off. It had been reported stolen by someone in Suffolk, that happened to work across the Bay from Newport News. Coincidence? Everyone thought naught.

The train wreck was rapidly followed by eyewitness reports of a man leaping out of the woods across from a gas station. A car veered into a tree and the driver died. Then the bus was hijacked by a single armed assailant, seen by the station attendant who quickly called the authorities.

The bus ride was one from hell, to hell. Three passengers survived the rain of bullets and the subsequent crash. All three had multiple gunshot wounds; one would probably die, one was in a coma, and the third would be disfigured for the rest of her life. Her disjointed story said a man, average everything, shot the driver and hijacked the bus. He fired wildly over his shoulder and people were screaming and dying all around her. At the scene of the crash, after the fire was extinguished, forensics found an Uzi and seven spent clips. Bullet holes were everywhere, through the seats, windows, and everything in between. Not a single unaccounted-for fingerprint on anything.

The police officer that had been chasing the bus believed that he saw a man leap out of the door of the moving vehicle. The man ran away clutching his left arm. He surmised the man had broken his arm after the jump and the subsequent abrupt stop as he plowed into a parked vehicle. The large dent in the passenger door of the car proved to be the point of impact, no clues were found at the scene. The officer felt his primary duties were to the people at the bus crash site, for the bus plowed into a group of people hanging out in front of a busy movie theater. The total dead in that accident was still rising as several people that were thrown from the impact and subsequent explosion were still dying.

Then, the very next day, someone reported finding a naked dead man in an alley. Clothes were located in a nearby dumpster that forensics quickly went to work on. It contained sea water residue and other known contaminants from the Chesapeake Bay. Only one man was reportedly seen on the bus and the clothes seemed to link him with everything in between.

Debbie groaned as she leaned over and grabbed a couple of pills off of her nightstand. She chased them down with a few sips of water and set the glass by the clock. She still had a lot of pain in her face and the news was adding to the confusion in her mind. Was this Garrett character the same one they were talking about? He was very average in height and weight. He was average looking but not a single scar marred his face, or hands. How could someone that deadly and that violently active survive unscathed? He certainly did not seem like a terrorist to her. He was too calm, too collected, and too well-disciplined. Fanatical terrorists had quirks, or she thought they must have. Why or how could someone easily and quickly kill six armed men and then take the time to have coffee with the shocked woman he had saved? It did not make sense. He did not make sense. More questions without answers.

Debbie picked up the phone and the crinkled business card that sat nearby. She dialed the number and looked at the clock, which displayed one fifty-two in the morning. She was about to hang up when the voice of a person wide awake caused her to pause.

"How are you, Debbie?"

"How did you know it was me?" asked Debbie as she wondered if she were being watched by him. A chill ran up her spine as she quickly looked to her window in a panic, trying to think of the various vantage points that lie outside of it.

"You're the only person I've given my card to in quite some time. Are you okay?"

"My face still hurts, and so does my head ... and my chest for that matter. I'm a mess. Who are you?"

"Get some sleep. We'll talk later," replied Garrett in a reassuring voice that calmed and relaxed her.

"Okay," said Debbie as she hung the phone up and fell asleep immediately. The television ran in the background but she was oblivious to it. The news repeated itself once again as the clues were examined and explained to those who may have missed it for the four thousandth time.

The ringing phone jerked her out of a peaceful sleep, which was the best she had had in many years. It was after ten in the morning and the television was still on. She glanced at the screen and it was the same broadcast as she had seen after midnight. It must have been a slow news day.

"Hello?" said Debbie, after picking up on the sixth ring.

"Hi Debbie, it's Mike."

"Hi Mike," replied Debbie as she lay her head against her pillow and closed her eyes. She really did not want to deal with him at the moment, but she had a feeling it was going to be one of those days. The pause lasted a lot longer than she expected and she began to wonder if Mike had asked her a question that she had missed. Her mind seemed to drift as she yawned and cringed as the pain from stretching her face hit her mind. She groaned quietly and looked out of her window as the sun finally showed itself.

"Are you okay?"

"My face hurts."

"I heard you had an interesting day after you left here. Did you find anything?"

"Damn, I had almost forgotten. At the crime scene I found a .22 projectile in the cement between two bricks. I never turned it in. I never did any paperwork for yesterday either. Oh God, I've got a busy desk day today." She groaned again, this time in response to all the work she could see piling up on her already overburdened desk. It was definitely a candidate for some gasoline and a match.

"I should be out of the hospital tomorrow and I can help with all of that," said Mike after another pause.

"Is your overly protective and somewhat psychotic girlfriend going to let you near me again?"

"Sister," replied Mike. "Half-sister. Secondary sister. Oh hell, my father's second wife's daughter outside of wedlock. She is somewhat psychotic and protective but I love her anyway."

"Oh," said Debbie, unsure of what else to say.

"She blames you for my being shot. She doesn't understand that shit happens in this job."

Debbie said nothing in response as she caressed her sore chest. It had been a few days since the shooting but it was still sore and would be for a while. With Kurt landing on her it did not help her recovery any, but that was the nature of her job, the unexpected always kept things interesting. She was not sure how long the silence lasted this time and wondered if she had fallen asleep again as Mike spoke.

"Are you still there?"

"Partly, my head still hurts from being a fist stopper for some Russian mafia asshole."

"Mafia? What kind of shit did we step into?"

"The worst kind. The kind that stinks for days. I've got to go and take a long shower, then get to work. There's just too much that needs to get done, so hurry up and get out of there, okay?"

"Now that's the Debbie I remember. Take care and I'll see you tomorrow."

"Okay Mike, you too."

She hung up the phone and slowly crawled out of bed. She stopped and looked at her battered naked body in her dresser mirror and wondered how she had ended up in this screwed up life of hers. Her torso and face were spotted with black-and-blue marks that would raise eyebrows wherever she went. If she were married her poor husband would probably be arrested for domestic violence. She chuckled in amusement at that thought as she entered the bathroom and turned on the shower. She stood under the hot water for several minutes while enjoying the pulsating spurts of water as they massaged her sore body. It was a refreshingly long shower that revitalized her.

Debbie dressed quickly and checked her weapon before snapping it into the shoulder holster. The bulge under her arm comforted her even though the gun was not of much use yesterday in the alley. Could she have prevented things from happening the way they had? Most likely not. The only thing that had saved her was the unknown man that came from nowhere. If Mike or any other detective had gone with her then they would probably both be dead. Only because she had been a woman was she abused by the mafia for as long as they had. They could confidently beat up a woman whereas a man they may have just killed outright because they were not as much fun to play with.

She entered the office and the detectives that were not currently busy flocked around her to gently squeeze her shoulder to let her know that they cared. Many people talking at once amounted to not a single thing being heard. She found herself nodding a lot in response. She would file the experience under *confusing* and gladly sighed when the crowd expended their energy and went back to their jobs.

Her desk was even more cluttered than she remembered and movement caught her eye. Leo motioned for her and she nodded. It was time to be grilled by the Lieutenant. She remembered the evidence she had found and removed it from her pocket. Once in his office she tossed the bag with the .22 round she had extracted from the alley onto his desk. "I found that at the crime scene, embedded in the cement between two bricks."

Leo picked up the bag and looked at it. "Great, I'll have it logged and analyzed." He placed the bag back on the desk and sat down on the corner to face her. "Sergei had two weapons on him, a Makarov in a shoulder holster and a .22 revolver on his hip. It was the murder weapon, forensics confirmed it sometime last night."

"Well, that's the evidence to solve this prostitute, or stripper, murder case," said Debbie as she sat down slowly.

"True, at least the *who* part, but now we need to know the *why*."

"Sergei hates women, or hated women. He used them and when he was done he'd discard them like trash."

"Where did you get this information?"

"Sergei told me right before he was going to throw me away just like the others," said Debbie as she carefully touched the bruise on her left cheek.

"How are you doing?" asked Leo as he stood and moved to sit down behind his large desk. He opened the drawer and pulled out a cigar before leaning back to look her over.

"Sore all over but otherwise okay."

"Good to hear. So who was the guy that took out the Russian mafia crew?"

"His name is Garrett Carmichael. Here's his card," replied Debbie, tossing the card onto the desk.

Leo picked it up and stared at it oddly. He hit the speaker button and heard the dial tone. He punched in the number and waited for the connection to be made. The phone began ringing and on the third ring it was answered by a woman.

"Stan's Flower Shop, a flower for all seasons. This is Sarah, how may I help you?"

"Hi Sarah, is there a Garrett Carmichael there?"

"No, sorry, wrong number."

"Okay," said Leo as he shook his head. "Thank you."

"Bye." The line clicked off and he tossed the card back to Debbie. It landed on the desk and she stared blankly at it.

"Bogus number," said Leo as he lit his cigar and leaned back in his chair. It creaked slightly and the blue smoke from the cigar drifted peacefully toward the ceiling fan.

"I called it last night and got him," said Debbie in her defense. "At least, I think I called him. Or maybe it was a painkiller-induced dream." She was beginning to doubt her memory for certain events. It had been a stressful day with one bizarre turn of events after another. Despite the restful sleep she thought she might have had she no longer felt rested.

"Well, try it now." Leo pushed the phone over to her. "Put it on speaker."

Debbie leaned forward in her chair, hit the speaker button, and then dialed the number. On the second ring the phone picked up and there was silence on the other end.

"Garrett?" asked Debbie. The pause was almost deafening before a deep voice that she recognized spoke.

"Hi Debbie ... and Leo? Is that right?"

Leo hit the mute button as he stood abruptly and opened his second desk drawer. "Damn, he's stalking you." He extracted a pair of binoculars and turned to his window, scanning the windows and tops of buildings nearby.

Debbie pressed the mute button and spoke carefully, "Yes, that's right."

"Now is not the time to talk. Let's meet later," said Garrett.

"Both of us?" asked Leo.

"No, just Debbie. You know, Leo, you should really stop smoking those things. They'll eventually kill you."

"That's what everyone keeps telling me," said Leo as he was drawing a blank in the windows or roof tops. That man had to have been within sight of the precinct. Maybe he had a high-powered sniper scope trained on him right this moment. That thought caused goosebumps to form on his arms and he hoped it was not true.

"Where do you want to meet?" asked Debbie.

"How about the same place we had coffee?"

"Okay, what time?"

"In an hour. I'd tell you to come alone but you won't listen. Leo has other plans though, but those binoculars might get you in trouble too."

"Why are you stalking my detective?" asked Leo as he gave up on his scan. He could find no one watching them from outside. At least nobody he could see.

"Who said that I was?"

The line clicked off and Debbie hit the speaker button to end the call. Things were becoming more bizarre by the minute. She looked to Leo who was visibly disturbed and began pacing back and forth across the small office. Debbie quietly shifted back to a normal sitting position and thought about the odd conversation. She was rather calm considering the disposition of the Lieutenant.

"We'll have the place crawling with cops. This shooter will be watching paint dry tonight in the county lockup. There's no way he'll get away from this one. He'll have to shoot the entire department. We'll need SWAT there too. I'll have the damn mayor call in the National Guard. He'll be knee deep in badges, so deep he won't be able to even walk without stepping on someone in a uniform ..."

The tirade would have continued for several minutes but Debbie burst out laughing. Leo looked at her and after several seconds he too began laughing. A few of the detectives looked into the office and wondered what was going on but went back to work.

"All right, I admit, I got a little carried away there," said Leo as he sat back down. "I just don't like feeling threatened, and in my own damn office. That guy gives me the creeps."

"He never threatened you, he was just watching us. Or had someone watching us." Debbie looked around the office and wondered if in this hi-tech world someone had placed a camera in there to watch them. It was possible. Some of the guys in the department specialized in that kind of surveillance. "Did he do anything wrong?"

"He shot and killed six suspects in a murder investigation. Isn't that enough?"

"He saved my life, isn't that enough?" shot Debbie in the mysterious man's defense.

"Debbie, you're like a daughter to me. There's just too much crazy shit going on in this world right now to let this guy go. We need to question him."

"You're the boss," said Debbie as she stood. "I guess I should finish some paperwork before I need to meet him at the coffee shop."

"Yeah, and I'll start getting the assets in place. We'll go down there in thirty minutes. I'll drive you."

"Yes daddy," said Debbie with a snicker.

Leo smiled and watched her walk out. She was not much older than his oldest daughter who was studying to be a grade-school English teacher, for which he was glad. The last thing he wanted his little girl doing was anything concerning law enforcement. It was a crazy job and Leo had already seen Debbie come close to death too many times for him to be able to sleep peacefully at night. He worried about her. He worried about all of the detectives under his command. It was a crazy world out there and the crazies were multiplying much quicker than the law-abiding citizens were. As each day went by the odds were growing against them. They were losing the battle.

CHAPTER
19

PHILADELPHIA PA

Garrett watched the coffee shop from a distance as the surrounding area began collecting plain-clothes officers. With five minutes to go he counted in excess of thirty cops scouting the streets below. The only thing damning that he did that they knew about were the six dead Russian mafia members in the alley. He was certain that they probably agreed that the world was a better place with them gone, even though their job was to arrest men like that. Him being here was insanity and there was no way that he would willfully put himself in that kind of jeopardy by entering the coffee shop. But his boss wanted him right at this very spot. It was important.

"Freeze, right where you are. Don't move a muscle because I'm a little bit trigger happy today," said the voice from behind him.

Garrett did not even bother to turn around. He continued to watch the circus below and waited for his boss to say something. The earpiece remained silent, which meant only one thing. What purpose did it serve with him locked up? Only his boss knew the answer to that one and it was not Garrett's place to question his boss.

"What's the problem?" asked Garrett.

"Did I tell you to speak?"

"No, you haven't said much of anything except telling me to freeze and that you want to shoot something. That doesn't exactly instill confidence in my having a future."

"Drop to your knees and put your hands on your head, fingers clasped and palms up."

Garrett complied and groaned when the man roughly forced him to the ground and tightened the zip ties on his wrists. The knee in his back was excessive but Garrett did not resist as he was searched.

"Whoa, we've got a big piece here, Sergeant," said the officer as he extracted the .45 caliber handgun. "Let's bring him in for questioning."

The trip to the station in the van was a long one despite the short distance. The questions continued to be fired at him but he kept staring straight ahead, answering nothing. From the line of questioning, someone or some group had linked him to every disaster along his path. Yes, modern technology was becoming quite troublesome when it came to his job. From the sounds of the evidence there was no way they could actually pin him for any of the disasters. It was all just suspicion and wild luck that they put one and one together in the first place. He still had up to six days left here. It was beginning to look like a very long six days.

The officers brought him into the station and searched him, making sure to collect and inventory every item he was carrying, which was not very much. He had the gun and holster, which was reported stolen in Oregon almost two years ago. A wad of cash, mostly twenties and totaling nearly eleven hundred dollars. The only other items of interest were a cell phone and earpiece.

"You like to travel light, huh? Where's your ID?" asked the officer filling out the arrest paperwork.

Garrett did not respond so the officer pushed him back in his chair.

The chair leaned back precariously and Garrett wrapped his fingers around the posts at the back, fully expecting to go over. He was still zip cuffed so he extended his legs to counterbalance his center of gravity.

"Did you hear me?" asked the officer.

"Yes, but I'm exercising my right to remain silent that you so dutifully gave me," replied Garrett. This angered the officer and he stormed away from the desk screaming for someone to remove him from there and get him into interrogation. Garrett found that things were going a lot easier than the last time he was arrested. Almost too easy.

Two officers showed up and took him to an interrogation room with a mirror on one wall and a window with bars over it on the other. They threw him into the chair and this time it did go over. Garrett groaned in discomfort but said nothing as the officers put the chair back up and seated him in it. They slammed the door shut behind themselves when they left.

It was coming and he knew it. He did not bother looking around and remained perfectly still as he stared at the door. He slowed his breathing down and relaxed as he began meditating. When the door opened once again he saw Debbie and Leo standing there with the annoyed officer.

"He's not talking," said the officer. "You can deal with him because I've had enough."

"Sure, no problem," said Leo as he shook his head at the officer. People like that gave the department a bad name and Leo was sick of it. He pulled out the second chair in the room and motioned for Debbie to have a seat.

"Who are you?" asked Leo as he leaned against the mirror, hoping to annoy at least one of the officers behind it.

"You already know the answer to that question," replied Garrett.

"You have no ID," started Leo as he opened a folder and removed the single sheet of paper within. "We ran your fingerprints and they match a ninety year old Korean woman that killed two police officers with a broken plate and was executed nearly twenty years ago. How is that possible?"

"Cruel coincidence," shot Garrett with a neutral expression on his face.

"To further confuse matters, the gun that was in your possession was reported stolen from Oregon two years ago. The only prints we could get from it were from a man found naked and dead in an alley on the other side of town. Do you know anything about that?"

"He didn't need it anymore."

"Did you get that money from him too?"

"Yes, same reason."

"After you killed him and stole his clothes?"

"He was dead inside long before I met him."

"So, it was just opportunity that led you to robbing him?" asked Leo, watching the man carefully for unspoken answers to his questions.

"No, necessity."

"You needed his clothes, his money, and his gun? Why?"

Garrett shifted his gaze to the plainly beautiful yet battered woman sitting across the table. He looked deeply into her soft brown eyes and felt comfort in her. She was an enigma to him and his concern for her he found to be an oddity in his life.

"To save Debbie."

"Bullshit. That piece of shit you robbed was found hours before Debbie even decided to enter that alleyway. How could you have known then that you were to save her?"

"I didn't. One must always be prepared for the unexpected."

"Why did you save me?" asked Debbie, really wanting to know. She was fairly certain that she had already asked him this question but she needed to know, or to hear it again.

"My boss told me to."

"Who is your boss?" asked Debbie.

"That is not information you can know at this time."

"Do you communicate with him on your cell phone?" asked Leo with a smile.

"Yes."

"It has a dead battery," said Leo.

"That does not surprise me," replied Garrett.

"What is his phone number?"

"Also information you cannot know."

"As soon as we bring power to that thing we'll extract it from the logs. You can help yourself by answering our questions. The more you hide and we have to extract the worse things will be for you in the long run," said Leo as he approached the table and threw the folder onto it. "Who do you work for?"

Garrett shook his head. There was no way he would ever divulge that information unless specifically given instructions to the contrary. It had never happened before and he doubted it would happen anytime soon, if ever.

"Did you kill all those people on the plane, two ships, a train and a bus?" asked Debbie.

Garrett looked at her but did not answer, he was done with this line of questioning. His face became a completely neutral blank slate. No emotions showed as he waited for the next question to be ignored.

"What organization do you belong to?" asked Leo.

Garrett turned and looked at Leo but did not answer.

"Exercising your rights again?"

"Silence is golden," replied Garrett.

Leo opened the door and called the duty officer over. "Put him in a cell overnight. We'll be back in the morning to see if he is more willing to talk then."

"Yes sir," replied the officer as he escorted Garrett from the room.

Debbie stood and walked to the door while carefully watching Garrett. As he passed her she reached out and grabbed Garrett's upper arm, stopping him. He turned and looked down into her warm brown eyes.

She opened her mouth to talk but said nothing and he smiled in response. The tension instantly left her body.

"It will be okay," said Garrett, not really specifying what *it* was.

The officer led him from the room and down the long hallway into the detention area. He then snipped the cuffs off while another officer opened the cell door for him. Garrett walked in and stood by the door, slowly looking over his new friends and quickly assessing their combat value. Only about half of them would be able to present a nuisance while the rest were of no consequence. None of those in the cell did Garrett consider a threat but he built his list anyway, mostly out of habit. The door closed behind him and the two guards laughed as they left. "Play nice now, you hear?"

"This is a bad idea," started Garrett as he examined all the eyes looking at him. "A very bad idea."

*

"What the hell do you make of that?" asked the Captain as he entered the room. He had been behind the mirror the entire time, watching the interaction.

"Not sure," replied Leo as Debbie sat down slowly. "He's so calm about all of this, it's driving me crazy. I've never seen anyone so at peace with his surroundings. It's scaring the crap out of me."

"He's just a punk. The other bitches in the cell with him will straighten his ass out in a hurry," said the Captain confidently.

"I'd keep a careful eye on him all night."

"What the hell for?"

"My instincts tell me that you'll need an ambulance before morning comes," said Leo as he took a seat across from Debbie. "Several of them."

"Listen up Lieutenant, you do your job and I'll do mine, okay? I've been here twenty-seven years. I know a punk when I see one."

"Fine. We'll be back in the morning. Come on Debbie, we've got some paperwork to do."

"Yes sir," replied Debbie as the two of them left the interrogation room and the building. Leo continued to shake his head in disagreement as he walked past the Captain.

*

It happened after the midnight shift change and the guard's walk-through inspection of the detention area. The biggest man in the cell approached Garrett quietly and kicked the bottom of his right foot. Garrett slowly opened his eyes and looked up at the big man. He was a beast of man and of possibly Puerto Rican descent.

"You're in my seat."

"I thought you were sitting over there," replied Garrett quietly while motioning with his head.

"After midnight I sit here."

Garrett stood from the bench and walked to another vacant seat, but was being followed by the big man. Garrett looked to him and the man shook his head slowly. Garrett pointed to a different seat and it was the same thing. He found a vacant spot on the floor near the cell door and sat down. The big man walked over and kicked his foot again.

"Not there either."

"Want me to remain standing?" asked Garrett politely.

"No, I think I want to kick your ass, stuff you into the toilet, and take a big shit on you," replied the big man as he punched his open fist.

"Not a very good plan for your longevity," said Garrett as he stood. The big man stood half a foot taller than him and was almost twice as big around. The man had no hair and a thick bushy mustache of dark black hair. He had not shaved in probably a week and had several scars on his neck. Without his boss giving him any further instructions, Garrett would need to rely on instinct and react accordingly. "Why don't you just go sit down and leave me alone."

"I don't like you," said the big man in Spanish.

The rest of the prisoners quietly awakened the others so they could watch the fight. Not a single person made any sound since they knew any cheers would result in the fight being stopped prematurely. It was not that often that a good fight occupied them more than a few minutes, because the excitement usually prompted someone to make enough noise to alert the guards.

"Leave me alone or I will send you straight to hell," replied Garrett in Spanish as he tensed for action.

The big man took a swing at him but Garrett moved slightly right as the man's hand struck one of the bars at full force. The man grunted in pain but kept coming at Garrett. This was not part of the plan. At least, as far as he knew. But, sometimes the unexpected *was* part of the plan. This confrontation was just not on his list of missions for his current plan. Oddly enough, his current line of thought was more of a concern to him than the large aggressor in front of him was. All Garrett could do was use his training and deal with his current circumstances as best he could, easily dodging another swing.

"Two," said Garrett as he readied for another attack. The rest of the cell occupants sat in silent anticipation, expecting a very one-sided fight in favor of the big guy.

The big man swung again and Garrett dodged to the side and punched the man in the sternum as hard as he could. A loud crunch echoed in the quiet dim light of the detention center as the big man collapsed to the floor.

"Strike three, you're out," said Garrett in English as he looked around at his other cell mates. "Does anyone else want to join him? There is still a lot of room left in hell."

No one answered, nor did they want to continue looking at the average-sized man that had just killed a much bigger man with a single punch. A few looked on in horror at the newly created corpse in the middle of the cell's floor. The big man had been an asshole and deserved his fate so they wanted nothing to do with the events. Several went back to sleep as Garrett returned to his original seat and crossed his arms in front of himself. He closed his eyes but waited for another attempt. There was still a lot of ego left in the room, he could smell it. That and fear were the strongest of the smells around him, although the toilet contained some smell that even he feared to investigate.

Hours later he awakened with struggling fingers wrapped around his throat, trying to squeeze the life out of him. There were at least three sets of hands intent upon killing him, the current reason was unknown. A quick assessment of his situation made him grasp the two nearest people by the testicles and twist while compressing. Two men screamed out in pain and released their grips while the third took a knee to his groin. Garrett considered it fighting dirty but all fighting was dirty so what was the difference. When fighting, it was always best to use whatever tactics benefited you and exploited a weakness in your opponent.

The three men struggled to regain their senses before they charged him. This time the cell broke out in chanting *fight* at the top of their lungs. Garrett jumped up and kicked out as the group closed in. The first man took a foot to the mandible and his jaw shattered with a loud snap. Garrett punched the man in the face and his skull cracked open to end his useless existence. The other two men threw punches and connected with Garrett's head and stomach. They fought wildly and without skill so Garrett grabbed the person on the right by the neck, putting him into a headlock, and lifted him quickly. Another snap echoed in the cell and several inmates gasped as blood sprayed out of the hole that the broken spine made at the back of the man's neck.

The last man hit Garrett in the nose and bloodied it. Garrett did not bother wiping the blood from his face, nor had the attack changed his demeanor in any way. Garrett ignored the blood and the pain as he grabbed the man by the arm and swiftly broke it just below the elbow. A swift kick broke the man's right leg at the knee. Another kick to the face broke the man's nose and a quick toss sent him headfirst into the cement wall. The sickened thud silenced several inmates as they began throwing up.

Sensing the situation was about to get even worse, Garrett prepared himself as another five men charged him. He could feel the hatred emanate from them and wondered what drove these men to kill themselves. He grabbed the nearest one by the arm and pulled as he kicked into the man's side. The loud sound of bones snapping rang out as part of the man's rib cage went into his lungs and heart, ending his life before he could even gasp out in pain or surprise.

The other four jumped on top of him, pinning his back against the bench, and began pummeling his face and chest. Garrett used the thumb from his right hand to grab the head of the man on his right like a bowling ball, his thumb making a hole of the man's left eye. A blood-curdling scream of anguish ran shivers down the spines of those nearby as Garrett jerked and snapped the man's neck.

He let go of the head as he picked his next victim. A quick knee to the groin lifted the man that was punching him in the head and allowed Garrett to deliver a shocking punch to his sternum. A forceful right elbow to the man's lower left chest broke a single rib bone off and sent it into several of his vital organs.

Garrett rolled off the bench and landed on the dead man he had just killed. He stood and lifted one of the remaining men by the neck with his left hand as he grabbed the right hand of the man that had just punched him in the gut. He used the man in his left hand to break the arm of the man whose hand he held with his right. After the solid snap, he increased his grip and sent another shower of blood on himself and others in the cell by ripping the man's throat out. He left that one to gargle his own blood and suffer a painfully slower death than the rest as the other one crawled backward away from him.

"Please don't kill me," whimpered the man as he begged for mercy.

The other inmates quickly moved away as Garrett approached the man and punched him squarely in the face. The man's body jerked back and his skull cracked against the bars, ending his life in a pool of his own blood.

Garrett could smell the fear now, and the smell of blood was even stronger as he assessed the carnage around him. He lost count of the lives he had just ended. He was not sent here for this and unfortunately his fate would soon be sealed by humanity. An alarm sounded and the lights came on as Garrett turned to look into the camera that had monitored the entire event. He was half covered in blood and the other half in sweat. His breathing relaxed as he stood there, waiting for what would come next. It would be a very long six days indeed.

The guards rushed in with pistols or riot guns trained on the man standing at the center of the cell. Blood and broken bodies made the holding cell look like an abattoir. Grown men, previous enemies, held each other and cried in fear at the horror they had just witnessed. Garrett raised his blood-covered hands slowly.

"You better move me into solitary before I am forced to finish off the rest of them," said Garrett, more of a command than a comment.

A young guard gagged reflexively and his muscles tensed, causing him to squeeze his trigger and fire, and the bullet struck Garrett in the abdomen. Garrett clutched the wound and dropped to the floor while other guards called a cease-fire and detained the young guard. The young guard buckled over and vomited on the floor in front of himself and several other guards did the same once seeing the grisly scene.

CHAPTER
20

PHILADELPHIA PA

W hat the hell happened here last night?" asked Leo as he and Debbie watched the cleaning crew and covered their noses. The detectives on night duty had spent hours sorting through the mess in the detention cell. There were blood splatters literally everywhere, including the ceiling of the cell. Once dead the victims evacuated their bowels thus adding to the vile smell encompassing the room.

"You didn't see the video feed?" asked the Captain as he watched both of them shake their heads slowly. He began walking to the door. "You won't believe it."

"I warned you about him," said Leo as he followed.

"Don't remind me."

Once clear of the area they removed their hands from their noses and returned to normal breathing. They entered the surveillance office and the officer on duty acknowledged them with a slight nod. He was young with very short brown hair and tired eyes that showed he had been at work on this tape for a very long time. He cued the tape in the machine for playback and looked at them to issue a brief warning. "Hold your stomachs and keep your vomiting to yourselves," said the technician, meaning every word of it.

The video played back with Garrett trying to avoid a fight against a much larger man. He tried to attain a peaceful resolution but the big man would have none of that.

"It all started here," said the Captain as he pointed mostly by habit than out of any usefulness. "Your prisoner tried to avoid a fight but Jorge pressed him."

They watched the short fight and Debbie gasped at the abruptness of the big man's death. She knew Garrett was a killer, she had seen him shoot six men faster than she could have drawn her gun. But killing with your bare hands was something completely different. Something personal.

"If that shocked you, you may not want to continue watching," said the Captain. "It gets worse, much worse. About two hours later three men decided to kill him in his sleep. Then after their deaths five more joined in."

The tape played several seconds of scrambled video and then cleaned up as the time stamp advanced. Debbie had to close her eyes when the blood started spurting. That was more than enough for her to take in one day. It was tough to watch such a stone-cold killer at work, barehanded, and taking on several attackers at once. He never wavered in his methodical approach to eliminating a threat.

"What the hell was that? One of your guys shot him?" said an angry Leo as he pointed at the screen.

"Yeah, a new guy. Just out of the academy. When he convulsed to vomit he accidentally squeezed the trigger and shot your prisoner in the gut. The round went right through but he required immediate surgery."

"Is he still at the hospital?"

"Yes, under guard, six of them. Two in the room, two outside the room, and two down the hall. If he so much as sneezes he'll be a dead man," replied the Captain.

"But it was all in self-defense," shot Debbie as she instinctively defended the man who had saved her.

"The D.A. is going to have a field day with this one," said the Captain as he yawned after a very long morning. "Your prisoner just cleared out his docket for the next week. He'll have lots of time to spend prosecuting him."

"Prosecute for self-defense? With witnesses and video?" shot Debbie. She knew the law as much as anyone else. "About the only thing you can get him on that would stick is carrying a concealed weapon without a permit. Everything else is debatable."

The Captain shook his head but did not say anything. Leo saw the look in her eyes and knew there would be no swaying her opinion. For things like this it was better left for the courts to decide. As flawed as the legal system might be, it was all they had to work with.

"I'm going to the hospital," said Debbie.

"Stay away from my prisoner," shot the Captain.

"Wrong, he's still my prisoner," replied Leo as he followed Debbie out the door.

As soon as they were out of earshot the technician ejected the tape. "We should let this guy loose on the prison system. There would be no more overcrowding."

"That's your best idea yet," said the Captain as he left the room. He still had paperwork to complete concerning this mess and the mayor wanted to talk with him.

*

Debbie entered the room as Kurt looked up and a large smile grew on his face. He looked the same to her as he had before, yet something was different about him now. It only took a few seconds before the look on her face changed Kurt's smile to a frown. He had seen that look before on many people, himself included. The last time he could recall was in the desert after a particularly gruesome encounter.

"It wasn't me," shot Kurt defensively, which caught Debbie off guard and caused her to smile. "Success."

"Success for what?"

"Getting you to smile."

Debbie shook her head slowly as she approached his bed and sat down next to him. She remained silent for several minutes and Kurt just stared at her, not saying a word. He brushed the hair away from her right eye and put it behind her ear. She continued to stare at the far wall so he placed his right hand over her hands, which were clasped in her lap. Her face was battered and bruised but he could see the pained confusion there was being caused by something else.

"How can someone kill nine people with their bare hands, while in a holding cell at a police station?" She never expected an answer. She did not even know if she wanted one, but a few seconds later Kurt spoke.

"Necessity."

"Necessity?"

"Or desperation, or psychosis, or who knows what else. It depends a lot on the person and the circumstance."

"Can you kill someone with your bare hands?" asked Debbie as she turned to look him in the eyes.

"Yes I can, and I have. Never nine at once, but I once had to take on two," replied Kurt carefully. When she did not reply or ask for further information he fought an internal struggle as he stared into her sad brown eyes. Something melted inside of him and he decided to continue, but not for her, for him. "I had just returned from Iraq and went out drinking with some friends. An altercation transpired between a good friend of mine and a drunk patron who pulled a knife. The drunk's friend joined in and I tried to break it up, but the first man stabbed me in the gut. Instinctively I broke his arm and shortly after that a chair hit me in the back. The man with the broken arm began beating my head with a chair leg so I stopped him, permanently. His friend didn't like that and drew a gun. In the ensuing struggle one of my friends took a round to the leg. I broke that man's neck before I realized what I had done."

Debbie continued to stare at him, barely blinking as she absorbed the data. She watched his strong facial expression weaken and turn to one of sincere regret. The internal struggle continued as Debbie watched in silence. She removed her hands from beneath his and rested them on top, softly squeezing it in comfort.

"For me," began Kurt as he lowered his eyes to stare at her small soft hands. "I ... I was back in Iraq at that moment. I had killed many in the war, a few at point blank range as I looked into their eyes and saw the shock and fear as the life bled from them. A marine is trained to kill instinctively and without hesitation when the situation calls for it. I tried to stop them but those two men started a dormant machine of war when that knife came out. I tried to diffuse the situation but they kept pressing, my instincts and training kicked in, and both lost their lives for it."

Kurt sighed heavily and leaned back against the pillow of his bed with tears forming in his eyes. Those were memories that he preferred to suppress and forget about, forever. But there was something in Debbie's eyes that silently begged to hear that. Not just to know more about him but to help her through the current dilemma that troubled her. It had been the most troubling part of his life and the court decided that, even though he was a decorated United States Marine, he needed some time behind bars and even more time in anger management classes. They also threw in many sessions with shrinks, which he abhorred. How could some dumbass civilian child, barely old enough to drink legally, even begin to understand the inner workings of the mind of a warrior? He tensed as the memory flushed the sorrow out by sending a wave of anger through his system.

A light squeeze from Debbie's hands pulled him back to the present. "I'm sorry," said Debbie quickly. "I didn't mean to ..."

"Don't worry about it," said Kurt quickly while cutting her off. He shook his head and rotated his hand to squeeze her hands gently as he looked into her eyes. "Why does this man confuse you so much?"

"He saved me a couple of days ago," said Debbie as she proceeded to tell Kurt about her near death experience in the alley. Then the phone call, the capture, the interrogation, and the entire grisly detention cell massacre. "Ever since I took that bullet to my trauma plate I've felt like my life is out of control," said Debbie as she looked at the floor. "It's almost as if Death is just sitting there watching and waiting for me, and I'm scared."

"I saw Death once," said Kurt, as the painful memory surfaced. "I told you before about the tank round hitting my buddy. Well, I dropped in a pool of my own blood. It got cold in a hurry. A medic was following me so closely he was almost in my pocket, and that's the only reason I lived through that one. My heart had stopped at one point too. Two of my buddies performed CPR while the medic quickly sewed some of my organs shut. I probably should have died right there, but I didn't.

"When it's your time to go there won't be a damn thing you can do about it. So you can't think that way or you'll bring about your own death through inaction."

Debbie nodded absently and stood slowly. Part of her dreaded the next visit but she needed to do it for both personal and professional reasons. She leaned toward Kurt and rubbed his chest as she kissed him quickly on the lips. "Thank you," said Debbie as she pulled away and headed for the door.

"Watch your back," said Kurt as she disappeared out the door. She was a very troubled lady and he hoped that the stories of his past helped her through whatever crisis she was currently dealing with. Maybe it was a way for him to work through them as well, so that they no longer haunted him. He could only hope. The first was a black spot on his soul that he struggled with as he tried to justify his actions. Had he done everything he possibly could have to prevent what had occurred? Every night spent alone he went through the series of events as he analyzed them one at a time. Would he ever be free of that pain?

*

"You can't go in there," said the officer on duty standing outside the door.

"But he's my prisoner," said Debbie in her defense.

"Doesn't matter, I have specific instructions from the Captain."

"It's okay," said Leo as he walked up behind her. "We'll both be going in."

"Yes Lieutenant, the Captain did okay you."

The officer allowed them to pass and the two guards within the room watched them enter. Both of them stood with their backs against the wall watching the single bed with Garrett resting in it.

"You are one dangerous individual," said Leo as he stopped five feet from the bed. He wondered if that was enough of a distance if the man decided to rush him.

"Yes, I am," replied Garrett, his expression remaining neutral.

"You killed nine prisoners," shot Leo.

"They attacked me."

"We found some of their guts on the ceiling fan."

"It was self-defense."

"If the guards didn't show up, would you have killed them all?"

"They were all dead inside anyway. If they wanted to die I would have obliged them," said Garrett without emotion. He was as calm as a monk having a beer on the beach at sunset.

"Did your boss tell you to kill them?"

"You had my phone," said Garrett in quick response.

"So you killed those men without his approval?"

"I kill when necessity dictates, or when I am ordered to."

"So, you are a contract killer?"

"I do not get paid to kill."

"What do you get?"

"It is my job."

"But as a job, you must get paid, right?"

"No."

"So you have a job that you do, killing people, and you don't get paid for it. Right?"

"Yes."

"What the hell kind of job is that?"

"A volunteer job."

"So you volunteered to kill people just for the fun of it?"

"I find no enjoyment in killing, but sometimes it has to be done."

"You didn't enjoy your little massacre last night?"

"No, I did not."

Debbie remained quiet and watched Garrett's face. His expression was completely neutral. No anger, no fear, and no concern. No emotion whatsoever. Leo and Garrett could have been having a conversation about the weather or an old high school reunion. Debbie could see Leo becoming agitated by his line of questioning and decided it was time to stop him before things got ugly.

"Leo," said Debbie sharply, which caused him to pause before firing off his next question. It was her turn for some questions. "Can I speak with him alone?"

"Are you crazy?" shot Leo as he turned quickly to face her.

"Yes," replied Debbie with a smile.

Leo turned to face Garrett and raised an accusing finger at him. "If you so much as even think about touching her I will kill you myself, with my bare hands. Understand?"

"Yes, sir," replied Garrett.

Leo reached into his pocket and pulled out the man's cell phone and earpiece. He tossed them onto the bed near Garrett and watched him lower his head to look at them.

"What does your boss say now?" asked Leo.

Garrett picked up the cell phone and placed the earpiece in his left ear. He held the phone in his left hand and looked right into Leo's eyes, pausing briefly before answering. "Not much, the battery is still dead."

"We put power to that thing and there wasn't a phone number to be found in it. The recently called and received lists were both blank and the address book was empty. It didn't even have your own phone number in it and the phone company has no record for you. I think your mind is whacked out of its socket and you are hearing voices that tell you to kill people."

Garrett stared blankly at Leo while his expression never changed. Leo waited for some kind of response or reaction but the man in the bed had chosen that moment to remain silent. Leo fumed for another handful of seconds before he sighed in disgust and turned abruptly to exit the room.

"Leo, take the guards with you. I want to talk with Garrett alone," said Debbie while still looking at the man sitting calmly on the bed.

"No, Debbie," replied Leo forcefully.

"Leo." Debbie turned and looked at Leo and he melted.

Leo saw the determination in her eyes and face and knew there would be no arguing with her. Her mind was made up and had been for quite some time. Besides, if this man had wanted her dead, then why did he save her in the alley? Leaving her alone with him was probably against some regulation somewhere, but it would not be the first time he bent the rules.

"Come with me," said Leo to the guards. They reluctantly followed him out the door.

The door closed with a click and Debbie turned to face Garrett, who remained unmoving on the bed. The silence continued as neither wanted to break the spell which encompassed the room. Several minutes passed and a bird landing on the edge of the closed window broke the silence with a single peck to the glass.

"Any further questions would be a waste of breath," said Debbie as she stood there with her shoulders slumped. There was nothing else she could do and seriously wondered why she was even there in that room. Nothing made sense to her anymore. The utter futility of existence crushed down upon her as she stood like a stone statue in front of a man she knew to be both a killer and a savior.

"Perhaps," replied Garrett in a near whisper.

"What should I do?" asked Debbie, not expecting an answer.

"Some questions do not have simple answers."

"Last week everything was so clear, but now I can't see a foot in front of my own face. I'm scared."

Garrett's eyes opened wide when the voice spoke a single word in Latin in his earpiece, "Leave."

Garrett flung the sheets aside and stood up. He felt nearly naked wearing the hospital gown as he slowly approached Debbie. She did not flinch nor did she react to his movement.

"Debbie, I need to leave," said Garrett as he stopped in front of her. "Right now."

"Okay," she replied before she realized it. "Wait." Debbie removed her coat, unstrapped her shoulder holster, and handed it to Garrett before she even knew what she was doing.

Garrett took the weapon, with two spare clips, and hung it awkwardly around his neck. He gently grasped Debbie's head with both hands and tilted it back so he could look into her dark brown eyes. Seeing the confusion and the doubt was as plain as day. He searched for fear, anger, and hatred but found none of those within her. She was not afraid of him.

"We will meet again," said Garrett as he released her and picked up a chair. He tossed the chair at the window and the breaking glass scared the bird to flight. He was up on the window sill and on the ledge before the door had a chance to open. He calmly stepped through the broken glass with his bare feet as he found the drainage pipe that lead from the gutter above to the ground below. Garrett was at the bottom and half-way across the access road before Leo and four of the guards made it to the window.

"Damn it, you let him go," yelled Leo as he turned and ran to her. He grabbed her upper arms firmly and shook her from the daze. "Did he do some mumbo-jumbo on you?" She began to cry and Leo pulled her close, wrapping his arms around her so she could cry on his shoulder. "Shit."

One of the guards conversed rapidly over a radio telling of the escape and the prisoner's direction of flight. Units were dispatched for pursuit and an APB was issued for the man wearing a hospital gown. It would not take very long to catch him since that attire was a beacon as bright as day itself.

"Is there anything I need to know about your conversation with him?" asked Leo.

"I gave him my gun," replied Debbie into his shoulder.

"You're suspended until further notice," said Leo as he led her out the door. "I'm taking you home where you need to stay for a while and straighten out your head. You're off this investigation, permanently."

"Okay," she replied feebly between sobs.

CHAPTER
21

PHILADELPHIA PA

G arrett needed clothes and fast. He needed to disappear and his current clothing would give him away too easily. His stomach area where the bullet had penetrated was sore but the strain of running was neither excessive nor uncomfortable. Even if it were, it would not have mattered.

"Next house," said the voice in Latin.

Garrett changed direction as he approached the back door rapidly. His bare foot impacted the door next to the handle and it separated from the frame. The loud crack of splintered wood caused a scream from within. He entered through the kitchen which showed disarray. The tenant was not too tidy of a person and piles of plates collected in the sink. Garrett crossed into the living room and found the source of the scream, a young mother and her two children huddled together on the couch watching cartoons. She was in her mid-thirties and appeared tired and a lot older than that.

She saw the gun hanging around his neck and gasped. "Please don't hurt my children."

"Quiet, I need clothes," said Garrett in a commanding voice. The children began crying and she stood, grabbing them one by one and placing them both in a playpen near the couch. She then ran to the next room with Garrett close behind and led him to her bedroom. This too was a mess, with dirty clothes strewn about the floor and the bed unmade. She opened the closet door to reveal quite a cache of male clothing.

"Take whatever you want," said the woman while crying and backing away slowly. "Do whatever you want to me, just don't hurt my children."

Garrett grunted in disgust as he grabbed a pair of neatly pressed jeans from a hanger. He shook them briefly and a cloud of dust grew in the air around him. The man in her life must have been long gone for any number of reasons. That explained the disarray, or possibly the disarray was the reason behind his leaving. Garrett did not care and he did not have the time or want to care about this woman. She was providing the clothing he needed to make his escape and nothing more. "Lie down on the bed and close your eyes."

The woman complied and kept crying which annoyed Garrett for some strange reason. The pants fit near perfectly so he grabbed a dark blue tee shirt, shook the dust off of it, and threw it on the bed next to her. He also took a brown jacket in a similar condition and a pair of brown work boots, possibly brown from the dust. Garrett removed the holster from around his neck and took off the hospital gown, throwing it to the floor to be lost in the rest of the clothing piles. He put on the shirt and boots, which were only slightly bigger than his feet. The jacket was the last thing he put on before picking the holster up.

"Don't hurt my children," pleaded the woman once again.

"You just can't be quiet, can you?" asked Garrett, not expecting an answer nor giving her the time to emit one. "All I want are these clothes. No pain, no sex, and no killing. So be quiet and let me work."

The holster was for a lefty, which was his usually favored hand, but it was configured for a much smaller frame. After the bus crash had weakened his left arm he had been favoring his right. He did not want to take the time to resize it so he extracted the firearm and magazines from it. He put the gun in his right coat pocket and the clips in the left.

The woman was crying when Garrett sat down beside her and gently grabbed her by the jaw. She opened her eyes and he tilted her head to the side so he could look into them and she into his. A shiver ran down her spine causing her entire body to shake in fear.

"Do you like nightmares?" asked Garrett softly.

"No."

"Then go to sleep for an hour and dream of happy things, like chocolate, okay?"

The woman's mumbled response exited her trembling lips and Garrett released her jaw. She fell asleep immediately as he stood and left the room.

The children were screaming and crying like their mother had been. Sensing that she was frightened and not knowing the reason why, they had joined in. The prolonged noise would attract attention so he approached the children rapidly and knelt beside the playpen to smile at them. "Be silent, little ones, and go to sleep," whispered Garrett. Both children complied immediately, grabbing blankets and rolling into fetal positions to enjoy an early nap.

Garrett stood and scanned the area as he walked out the broken back door, closing it behind him. He looked both ways and then ran parallel to the hospital, crossing several streets before he came to a passenger exiting a taxi at the curb. Behind the taxi was a truck with an open back full of wooden boxes and Garrett jumped into the waiting vehicle. Wherever it was going was a much safer place than anywhere near the hospital. He contemplated leaving the city but his mission was not yet complete.

Several miles later the truck stopped at a light and Garrett chose that point to jump off and disappear in a crowded market area. He found an alleyway and slipped into the shadows, finding a nice quiet area to hide until dark. He watched the people walking by through an opening between a stack of boxes and the metal dumpster. This place smelled bad but it served a purpose for him. So he settled in and sat down to wait.

Almost eight hours later the sun began to set making it safer for him to move around. Shadows and movement in the dark were obscured, and a person was only a person if they strayed into the light. He had more than half a chance.

It took him over an hour of sneaking through the city to find what he was looking for. It was an apartment building amidst other apartment buildings, looking just like all of the rest on that street. The only way to tell them apart was by the number, and maybe the odd tree here or there. It was a brick-faced building standing four stories tall and covered with windows. The front of the building had steps going up to double doors and an intercom system that tried to maintain security.

Garrett watched the so-called security barely slow down a group of individuals as they kicked their way into the building. The muted thumps of several silencers going off could not be confused with any other sound on the planet. He watched a couple of people get slaughtered as the group of four ascended the staircase. They were wearing black, which was wasted in the full lighting of a living facility. The MAC-11 machine guns held at the ready would not be a match for anyone within those walls, including their primary target somewhere above. He needed to even the odds and sensed that the four going in the front were not the only ones assaulting the building.

Garrett ran across the street and between the narrow slit to the right of that building. He made his way to the back of the apartment complex and found what he was looking for within seconds. The wires called to him as he removed the handgun from his right pocket. He was within point blank range when he fired several rounds to cut both power and phones. The three shots echoed loudly in the back alleyway, causing those within earshot to pause in their actions. Most people went right back to whatever they were doing, since gunshots were sometimes the norm in this area of town.

*

Debbie's eyes went wide when she was plunged into darkness and heard the unmistakable shots ring out. She grabbed her phone but it was dead, which did not comfort her any, and she had never wanted a cell phone either. She had been in the middle of watching some mind-less television, just to have something on in the background as she sat there thinking. Now her mind switched to the task of figuring out where her other gun was hidden. She rarely ever used it, except for the occasional target practice. It was a .22 caliber semi-automatic pistol that held ten rounds, and may only succeed in pissing an attacker off even more than he already was. Some well-placed shots with it could kill, but in darkness she may only draw attention to herself.

Her wandering thoughts were yanked back to reality when she heard the recently familiar Slavic language being spoken in the hallway outside of her apartment door. There was confusion out there, which she understood because she herself was rather confused. Debbie pulled herself up just as her door was kicked open and flashlights began to play around her apartment.

Silenced shots rang out and bullets peppered the furniture around her as at least two weapons switched to full automatic. Her television exploded sending glass shrapnel into the air and showering her with fragments as she dove to the floor behind the couch. She crawled rapid-ly to the kitchen and opened the utensil drawer she knew the location of by heart and extracted a long knife. The gunfire ceased and the flash-light continued to flicker its way around her living room.

More speaking in Russian between the two assailants gave their po-sitions away as they searched for her. Debbie knew they were after her to kill her, the coincidence was just too bizarre. Garrett had her gun, which left her rather naked considering the situation. *How convenient for the Russians*, thought Debbie. She seriously doubted that Garrett was working with them, but that possibility started to play itself out in her mind.

She chanced a glance around the counter as the lights played elsewhere in the room. One of the lights was coming her way while the other was heading to her bedroom. The light went over the counter and checked the kitchen as it progressed to her location. She tensed up with the knife in her left hand as she waited until she saw the attacker's leg. She plunged the knife into flesh and was greeted with a scream but did not wait to see what happened. She extracted the knife and stood while ramming it deeply at a forty-five degree angle upward into the man's midsection, right below the sternum. The blade pierced the man's heart, killing him instantly, and he dropped to the floor.

Debbie grabbed the flashlight and turned it off, then took the man's MAC-11. A glance to the hallway revealed a light coming back to the living room to check on his friend. A questioning voice in a language she did not understand elicited no response from the dead man. The question came louder as the flashlight found the corpse and Debbie ducked around the corner into the kitchen. Several silenced shots rang out and impacted her kitchen cabinets, ricocheting off of pots and pans, smashing plates and glasses, and ventilating her refrigerator with muted thumps. Debbie heard the slide lock as plain as day and the spent clip bounce off the floor before she acted. The man was occupied with reloading and never saw the small woman take careful aim at his flashlight and fire. She dumped half of her clip into him and was rewarded with grunts of shock and a loud thump of a body hitting the floor.

She took a chance at giving away her position but she had to know the attacker's status. She turned on the flashlight and found the corpse whose chest was riddled with bullets from the weapon that was deadly accurate at short range. She turned off the flashlight and searched for replacement clips on the body in front of her. Without pockets she held two in her right hand while the gun was in her left. There was no need for a flashlight anymore since she knew her apartment quite well. Depending upon how dead these guys wanted her there was the risk of a grenade being rolled into her midst. She hoped that was not the case. She also hoped that these killers needed the confirmation of a cold body to complete their contracts. How big was this can of worms that she had opened? That question still ran through her mind.

More flashlights approached and Debbie rapidly relocated to her hallway, with her bedroom behind her. She had a good bead on the door but no idea how many more were after her. That was when she remembered her police radio on the dresser in her room. She backed up slowly as a flashlight entered her apartment and light played around her living room. When the light found the two dead bodies on the floor the Russian conversations became rapid and increased in volume.

Debbie crouched low and tried to hold the weapon steady with her full right hand. When an attacker's flashlight appeared in her sights she aimed a little to the left and depressed the trigger. The silenced MAC-11 sprayed rounds accurately as the spent shells bounced off the wall next to her, clinking to the floor. The noise was a lot louder than she had hoped. Another attacker dropped dead but his friends showered her location with wild fire as they extinguished their flashlights. The muted muzzle flashes were all she saw as a round penetrated her right shoulder and sent her backward onto her ass.

The pain was intense and Debbie gritted her teeth as she ejected the spent clip and inserted another one. She racked the slide to put a round in the chamber as she pushed herself backward down the short hall. Another bullet grazed her left calf as she rounded the corner into her bedroom. Gunfire continued as another attacker took over so the first could reload. Debbie stood and grabbed her police radio, switching it on and holding the button down. Silenced shots rang out and thumped against the woodwork, causing glass lamps to shatter.

"Dispatch, Debbie Mason. Help, I'm under attack in my apartment.

Estimate half a dozen attackers with automatic weapons, need backup immediately."

"Understood detective. Help is on the way."

She turned off the radio as the gunfire paused and Debbie held her gun around the corner to dump half of her clip in their direction. She was rewarded with a pained shout as several of them returned fire. She was running out of room and was down to a clip and a half of ammunition, which was probably insufficient for the task. She moved between her bed and the window and began praying for backup to arrive. Her right shoulder hurt badly as she rested the MAC-11 on the bed and aimed it at her bedroom door. Moonlight streamed through her window, which probably gave away her position but she was painted into a corner. This would be her last stand.

A silhouette appeared in the hallway and she fired, finishing off the attacker and her current clip. She reloaded rapidly and fired off a few rounds to keep the attackers at bay as she tried to buy some time. How many were left?

*

Garrett entered the building through the back door, which had already been kicked off of its hinges. Several dead bodies of men, women, and children were littered about on the ground floor as he approached the staircase.

"Outside, fire escape, hurry," said the voice in Latin.

Garrett ran outside and jumped up to catch the lower ladder, bringing it down with his weight. He climbed rapidly to the roof and ran to the front of the building. There were a few old-fashioned television antennas scattered about and a door that led below. He made for the door but the voice spoke loudly, stopping him.

"No time, ten feet from the northwest edge, first window," said the voice urgently in Latin.

Garrett ripped several wires from the antenna farm and flung them over the edge of the building. He began scaling downward as muted shots rang out. His boss' sense of urgency caused his heart to race as he made his way down the wires to the small awaiting ledge outside the window. He glanced in and saw an attacker wearing black aiming a weapon down at the floor. The attacker fired a single shot and a female screamed out in pain as the weapon's slide locked back.

"Shit," said the man in Russian as two others entered the room.

Garrett fired at the closest assassin as the other two attackers saw him silhouetted against the outside light of the moon. He fired two rounds, one to break the window and the second to pass through the man's temples and lodge itself in the bathtub. The man dropped to the floor as Garrett leaped through the broken window. Both of the remaining men opened fire and Garrett's upper body and midsection were riddled with bullets. Garrett fired two rounds rapidly and both men dropped to the floor dead once the bullets entered their masked skulls.

"I really hate that," said Garrett under his breath as a trail of blood exited his mouth and rolled down his chin. He did not bother examining the forty-six entry wounds scattered about his torso, he could feel each and every one of them. He turned around and sat down on Debbie's bed, silently covering it with the blood leaking from his body.

"Thank you, again," said Debbie feebly.

"You're welcome," replied Garrett as his breathing became labored.

"What brings you here?"

"I had to return your gun," said Garrett as he placed her gun on the bed next to her pillow. "Thanks for letting me use it. It is a very accurate weapon."

"My pleasure," replied Debbie with a struggled smile. "But I don't think I'll have much use for it where I'm going."

"Where's that?"

"I'm going to die. The shoulder wound doesn't seem too bad but this other one, I think it hit my liver."

Garrett nodded slowly as sirens grew in the distance. He stared at Debbie's face in the moonlight. She was a pretty girl and she had a very strong will, a lot stronger than she gave herself credit for. The reflection of white, blue, and red lights flickered and danced over the walls of Debbie's bedroom. Garrett sat up straight and looked out the window as he took a deep breath. He placed his left hand on the bed beside him and it was instantly soaked with his blood. Several of the bullets had gone straight through him while others were lodged in various organs. He tried to count the points of pain but there were more than he had the time to contemplate.

"I'll see you later," said Garrett as he fell forward into a bloody pool on the floor at her feet.

Flashlights once again played on the surroundings as several officers flooded into her apartment. Debbie tried to scream out but was entranced by the unmoving body of Garrett that lay in front of her. He once again came to save her, but this time he died in the process. Why? She just could not understand the reason why. What was so special about her? Who was that man? There were too many questions without answers in her life and the pain in her body was beginning to fade. The last thing she remembered was the light hitting her face.

EPILOGUE

PHILADELPHIA PA

I t's about time you wake up," said Leo as he watched Debbie open her eyes. Her gaze was distant as she looked at him, or through him, he was not sure which. "I thought you were going to be asleep all day and I have work to do."

"Sorry to take you away from all that," replied Debbie weakly and half mumbled. The pain in her body was muted by the drugs that were dripping from the clear intravenous bag hanging near her bed. Her mind was very cloudy but she remembered the incident as if it were a dream, or a nightmare. If the attackers had waited just thirty minutes more she would have been naked and in bed. How much of a fight could she have put up under those conditions?

"Garrett was found at your feet, what happened?"

"I was out of ammo and looking down the smoking barrel of a silenced machine gun that had just slide locked. Then Garrett came smashing through the window and saved me from the Russian mafia ... again. How is he?"

"Oh, only about three kinds of dead," replied Leo as he sat down on the chair near the window. The words stuck in his throat as he tried to talk. He could feel the lump grow as he spoke the last word.

"Three kinds?" asked Debbie.

"Yeah, heart destroyed, both lungs perforated, and every internal organ punctured or shredded beyond repair. The autopsy recovered twenty-eight slugs from his body. He was dead long before he hit the floor."

"That's odd," replied Debbie as she tried to replay the scene in her bedroom through her mind. She remembered looking into the mask of the man behind that machine gun and seeing his annoyance at discovering a spent clip. Then shots rang out sending glass everywhere as Garrett entered through the window. The remaining assailants unleashed a fiery rain of bullets upon him, spraying the wall near the window with his blood. He looked so calm and never even flinched as projectiles penetrated his skin. He just casually raised her pistol and sent only two rounds in their direction to silence them. She never saw those other men go down but knew that they must have. He never missed, those were his words.

"What?" asked Leo.

"After he was shot he killed two attackers, then he sat down on my bed and talked with me for a minute or so."

"Impossible. Maybe you remembered it wrong."

"Possibly," replied Debbie, unsure of her own memory anymore. It had been an odd day, and an even odder week. It was easily the worst week of her entire life, taking all the previous bad things that had ever happened to her and combining them. She stared at the ceiling and wondered what had happened for her to deserve this and why, and she never heard the concerned voices around her.

"Debbie, are you all right?" asked Leo as he stood and rushed to her side. She looked pale and her eyes did not seem quite right. Another form rushed to her side and Leo acknowledged his presence.

"Hi Debbie, it's Kurt. How are you?"

"Kurt, I feel funny. I just need some rest," replied Debbie in a very weak voice. She turned to look at him and had problems focusing as she blinked in an attempt to clear the blurriness from her eyes. He looked so sad. "We can go for coffee later, okay?"

"Okay, I'll see you later then. Keep smiling, Pancake, you've got a pretty smile," said Kurt as he leaned over and kissed her on the forehead. As he moved to the door he looked back at her and struggled to keep the tears from flooding his eyes. She was such a strong person and someone that he wanted the time to know better, but that was never going to happen. He had seen people knocking at Death's door before and knew that her time was short.

Leo exited the room after him and both began walking down the hallway to the nurses station in silence. Both knew the look on her face and neither wanted to acknowledge it as fact. Both had seen it before, both were accustomed to death, but both also did not want her to go although the choice was neither of theirs to make.

"She doesn't look good," said Leo to break the silence.

"Her time is short," replied Kurt as he tried to distance himself from the situation, but failed. He cared about her more than he wanted to admit. That was the first time in a very long time that he felt like that about anybody. He had been running from his feelings for so very long and the best place he had ever found to hide was where everyone else was hiding from themselves. Being a bouncer at a strip club was more than just a job for him, it allowed him to avoid the answers and even the questions. No one that worked there ever asked any question that they feared would be asked of them. It was the perfect place to disappear, and that he had done well, until now. Now he did not need to hide anymore. He had finally found something worth living for and she was being yanked away from him. *Dammit!* He would find purpose in it though, he had to, she was worth it and he could not let her down. He knew the tears would start soon and he would forever miss her.

"Hey doc," said Leo as he called the doctor that had performed the surgery on her. "How is she?"

"Well, I won't sugarcoat it for you, it's just a matter of time. Her liver is a mess. That bullet shredded it up in a hurry and there is no way we could get a donor replacement in time. She passed the point of no return long before she arrived at the hospital. I'm sorry."

"Damn, I really didn't want to hear that," replied Leo as he looked to the floor. Kurt sighed as the doctor continued to describe her futile situation.

*

A man approached from the opposite direction and entered Debbie's room unseen. Garrett wore a doctor's smock and sat down on the bed beside Debbie, holding her right hand in his own. She opened her eyes slowly and stared at him in disbelief. She recalled hearing that he was dead but could not remember if that was a dream or reality. Was he really there? Was she? Not much made sense to her anymore. Everything was shrouded by a misty cloud of confusion. She smiled at him and closed her eyes.

"I heard you were dead," said Debbie in a whisper.

"Maybe I'm not, maybe I still am, or maybe I was never alive to begin with," replied Garrett as he caressed the back of her hand.

"Don't confuse me, I think I'm going to die soon."

"You are. Are you afraid?"

"Yes."

"Why?" asked Garrett out of curiosity.

"Because I don't know what to expect."

"It will be all right."

"How do you know?" asked Debbie, really wanting to believe him. He was such an enigma and thinking about him at this point was too much for her brain to comprehend.

"My boss told me so."

"Who is your boss?" she asked, realizing that it was the same question raised when he was arrested. A slight pause made her wonder if he would avoid it again.

"God," he answered with a smile.

She opened her eyes in surprise, definitely not expecting that response. "God?"

"The One and Only."

"But you killed people. Lots of them. Did you cause all of those so-called accidents? Did you kill everyone on the plane, both boats, the train, and the bus?"

"Yes, that's my job."

"It said 'CAD Specialist' on your card. What's a CAD Specialist? What's the SM Division? I thought it was all computer related, but that doesn't make much sense."

"Catastrophic Accidental Death Specialist, Soul Management Division."

"Soul Management? Are you the Grim Reaper?" Debbie's voice was becoming more mumbled but Garrett understood it just fine, almost as if reading her thoughts.

"My entire division is the Grim Reaper. We collect souls from all over creation. My specialty is in creating massive accidents that send many to the afterlife."

"But why? I don't understand why."

"The good go to Heaven and the bad go to Hell. Those that have minor defects in their souls go to Purgatory where they are cleansed and prepared for Heaven. Those that I kill are wanted immediately in the afterlife, but that isn't my main purpose. My main purpose is to affect the lives of those that know the people that I kill. It gives those people working their way into Hell a chance to realize this and atone for it. If they work at fixing their souls they will have a spot in Purgatory. Not everyone takes the chance I give them, but giving them that chance is why I exist."

Debbie tried to nod but could not move her head. There was not much life left in her and a part of Garrett was sad for her. Sad because everyone she knew and everyone she left behind would be hurt and saddened by her death. Her place in the universe was changing and he was happy for her for that. She was going to a much better place than this world.

"But why did you save me, twice? If I was to die why didn't you let me die earlier? Why didn't you kill me?"

"You needed to be here to change someone's life around, to give them a purpose or reason for living, to put them on the path that they needed to be on next. Your death alone would have been insufficient. A bond needed to be formed for your death to make a difference in his life. The time I gave you by saving your life allowed this to happen. He now has his chance at Purgatory."

"Who?"

"Kurt."

Debbie thought of that troubled man and of how much she cared about him. She did not really know him that well but from the talks that they had and the opening of his most deeply held secrets she instantly understood. It all made sense right then and there and she smiled. She was still afraid but there was nothing she could do about that. At least she helped someone before she had to leave this world.

"Almost time," said Garrett.

"I'm scared," mumbled Debbie.

"Don't be. I am here to help you across. I don't do this kind of work, it's not in my job description. But you are a very special case, you are a friend. It is time, Debbie. Purgatory beckons."

"Thank you," said Debbie as she squeezed his hand gently. Her eyes closed and she smiled as a wave of happiness and contentment pulsed through her body. Then she was gone from this world and her smile faded as did her life.

"My pleasure," said Garrett as the machine next to the bed flatlined and an alarm went off at the nurses station. Garrett stood and kissed

Debbie's forehead before he turned and hid in her bathroom. The door to her room opened rapidly as doctors, nurses, Leo, and Kurt ran in and to her side. Everyone was preoccupied with Debbie as Garrett slipped out behind them and into the hallway unnoticed. He walked down the hall at an even pace as a genuine smile of satisfaction crossed his face. She was in a much better place now and he felt honored to have helped her make the transition. In his specific line of work, most souls crossed rapidly and with fear and pain. He could do nothing about them, that was the way things worked. But she was special. This mission was special. This mission was different. This mission was done.

Paul J Belanger

was born in Western Massachusetts in 1966. He joined the Air Force at 18 as an aircraft electrician and became interested in aviation. In 1988 he began flying, earned his private pilot certificate in 1992, and moved to Colorado Springs to complete flight school. Paul currently lives in Maine where he is a flight instructor, charter pilot, and co-owner of a computer gaming software company, Lost Luggage Studios, with his brother Jamie.

www.ingramcontent.com/pod-product-compliance
Lightning Source LLC
Chambersburg PA
CBHW061208170626
46809CB00003B/1284